EARTH DRAGONS BOOK 2

CHARLENE HARTNADY

CHAPTER 1

Demi had the same dream every night. She dreamed about the day her sister died. It didn't matter that she hadn't been there when it happened. She still dreamed about it. Still lived it. Breathed it.

It was always the same dream. Terrifying and real. It was like she was actually sitting on the back seat of the car… like a ghost. Silent and unseen, unable to communicate, or to intervene. It didn't matter how hard she tried. How loud she screamed. It didn't work. The terrible events would keep unfolding. Keep playing out anyway.

Her sister's soon-to-be mate, Cody, was behind the wheel of the vehicle. His shoulders were relaxed, his hair glinted in the sun. He turned up the radio a little, grinning at her sister who smiled back. It was so real, so incredibly vivid. She could see the love shining in her sister's eyes. Demi couldn't hear what was playing through the speakers. Couldn't hear anything. She could only see. The tarred road stretched far ahead of them. She could see the mountains and how the road curved upwards.

She could see her sister. Her dark hair, long and thick. Her wide smile and bright eyes. Now Brie was laughing at something Cody was saying. So happy. So carefree. So utterly oblivious.

Demi closed her fists to keep from trying to reach out and touch her. She wanted to shake Cody. To try to let them know she was there. More than anything she wanted to warn them... but it wouldn't work. Any attempts would be futile. She'd tried countless times. She clenched her teeth to keep herself from screaming. If only they could hear her. She'd tell Cody to pull over. She'd tell him to stop the car. Most of all, she'd tell him to keep his eyes on the road.

Brie loved going into Sweetwater. She loved going shopping and eating at the restaurants. Her older sister was the strangest wolf shifter Demi had ever met. She preferred the town to the forest, and nice dresses to her fur. She preferred fancy restaurant food to cooking on an open fire. It was how she was wired. Different. Demi loved Brie for it.

Cody liked to indulge his female and so there they were, on their way back from one of their excursions. Joking and laughing. Cody's eyes straying from the road more and more often and for longer each time. They were headed deeper into the country. Maybe that's why he was less observant. She didn't like to use the word 'careless.' Didn't like to think negatively about the male, since he already beat himself up, doing a better job than anyone else could.

Brie put her hand on his jean-clad thigh and squeezed. Demi felt her heart beat faster. She could actually hear it pounding. Like the thing had migrated to her head. Her mouth felt dry. It tasted funny. She'd come to recognize it as fear. Intense. Extreme. Useless, like the adrenaline that coursed through her, all because there was nothing she could do.

Cody looked at Brie, his eyes softening, a smile toying with the edges of his mouth. He winked.

Demi felt tears building behind her eyes. Her throat hurt from *not* screaming. From holding it back. Her heart pounded even faster. Thumping like mad between her temples. So loud.

There wasn't much road left before the bend. The one that would take them up into the mountains. Cody looked straight ahead, this time he was laughing at something Brie had just said. They made the turn and then the next, winding their way up and up.

Her nerves were on edge. Although she gulped in air, she struggled to breathe. There was more laughing. More joking. They made such a stunning couple. The perfect couple. Everyone said so. They still did. The perfect couple destined to be together forever, only fate had different ideas.

"No," Demi whispered. "Please," she added, as she noticed how close they were to the next bend. It was *the* bend.

Neither of them heard her warning. Brie leaned over to Cody, her gaze sultry. She said something that made Cody give a half-smile. A special smile. One he only ever gave to Brie.

"Don't!" the word slipped out. She couldn't help it.

Cody began to turn the wheel as they neared the bend, his eyes moving from the road to Brie and back again. They were nearly through the turn when Cody caught Brie's lips with his. A quick brush which lasted all of two seconds. Two seconds too long.

On a normal day, it would have been absolutely fine. He had negotiated this road so many times. He said he knew it like the back of his hand. Said those words so many times since that day, she could actually hear them now. That and the pounding of her heart. Loud now. Thumping like a drum.

The couple in front of her were pulling back from their kiss. Demi could see the car coming at them. The pick-up was straddling the wrong side of the road. This was the part where things slowed down.

The other car held its course. There was no swerving. No braking. No reaction whatsoever. She knew from the report that those things hadn't happened, on account of there being no tire marks. The occupant of the other vehicle had more than likely been looking away as well. What were the chances of that? Neither driver was paying attention.

They'd never know for sure because the thirty-two-year-old, father of three died in the crash. Unfortunately, Cody *did* see the vehicle just before impact. He tried to swerve out of the way. If he'd maintained their current course… if he hadn't been looking away in the first place… maybe. But he *had* been looking away and his quick reflexes had only made things worse.

She watched as his mouth dropped open, his eyes taking on a desperate look, his hand closed tightly on the wheel as he yanked it to the right. To the sharp decline. To where the road gave way to a steep slope.

Brie screamed. Her eyes filling with terror. At this point in her dream, the sound would flare back up. She'd hear that scream. Piercing. Drowning out the screech of the tires as they locked. Then she'd hear the crunch as the side of Cody's vehicle connected with the other car. It ricocheted off, the impact causing them to careen over the edge.

Her sister's screams grew louder… more intense… more

terrified as the vehicle plunged downward. It picked up speed, the wheels barely touching the ground because of the severity of the slope.

Demi was screaming as well. She couldn't help it at this point. Her body jarred and jostled. Her head hit the roof as they crashed into something. A tree stump or a boulder. She wasn't sure of exactly what it was. The car began to roll and roll. It felt like she'd been tossed in a blender. Her head hit the side of the vehicle. Her sister's screams cut suddenly, replaced by laughter that turned her stomach. Louder and louder. Her stomach lurched just as everything went black.

Demi sat up in bed, she sucked in a deep breath as she did it. Her sheets were clutched tightly in her hands. Her eyes were wide, and she was panting. She could feel the dampness on her forehead.

Why?

Why did Brie have to die?

Why Brie?

She stopped herself there. Just as she did every time as she awoke from the nightmare. It took a few more seconds for her heart to slow down. For the terror to subside.

It was still dark outside. Demi knew that she could forget about sleep. She sighed and switched on the light next to her bed. She didn't need it, but it brought her comfort. She picked up the novel she was reading, noticing that she was already two-thirds of the way through it. A symptom of waking up hours before the rest of the world.

She groaned when she realized what day it was. Sunday. Not just a normal Sunday either. It was one of *those* Sundays. Demi had pretended to be sick two weeks ago. There was no way she was getting away with an excuse again. She groaned once more and pulled the covers over her head.

CHAPTER 2

So far so good.

How long would it last though? How long would they skirt around the one burning topic that she knew her father would want to discuss? She knew what it was because he brought it up every second week at their family lunch like clockwork. Even though she loved her family with all her heart, she'd been avoiding them more and more lately. Demi felt like she was perching on eggshells right then. Fragile ones that would break if she breathed too deeply. "Anyone for more potato salad?" She held up the bowl. She needed to work harder at keeping the conversation light. They could talk about food, the weather, anything other than *that*.

"Yes, please," her brother spoke around his food.

She passed the bowl to Cody who handed it to Serge. "Did you bring some? Please tell me you did." Serge raised his brows, a grin on his face.

Demi made a face at him. "I can't believe you're thinking about food while eating. That can't be possible."

Cody chuckled. "He's on his third helping as it is."

"I'm a growing male," Serge said, as he stuffed a forkful of food into his mouth.

Demi shook her head, looking down at her almost empty plate. She'd taken a second helping of potato salad. Her mom made the best salad this side of the mountains. She'd tried to make it herself, even followed the recipe to a 'T' but it didn't taste the same. "Of course you are." She laughed as well. Serge was twenty-three. Hardly a growing male anymore. She laughed harder as the whole table joined in. For just a second, it felt like old times, she glanced to her right. Looking for Brie.

Cody grinned down at her. Cody. Not Brie. Her breath caught as realization dawned. Cody's smile faltered. Had he realized the same thing? Had he caught himself too? He put his hand on her back and rubbed once in a brotherly gesture. "Demi brought cookies alright, but they're all mine," he said.

Cody's hand stayed where it was, making her feel awkward. He never left his hand there. Demi looked down at her plate and scooped up a mouthful of potato salad onto her fork. She moved forward but his hand stayed where it was.

"No damned way," Serge said. "Demi has been baking for me for years. Those cranberry biscuits are mine." Her brother looked back her way. "Are there chocolate chips in them?"

How she loved Serge. He didn't pick up on the discomfort that had descended on the table like a dark cloud. "You know there are." She smiled back.

"White chocolate?" His eyes widened. "Please tell me there are white chocolate chips in there. Lots of them."

"Oh, but of course. I added extra." She smiled, winking at him. Cody's hand felt hot and heavy. She wanted him to move it.

"They're mine, right?" Serge asked. "Not his." He pointed a thumb at Cody. "It won't be long, and he'll have all the cookies he wants since you guys will… " He finally realized how uncomfortable things had become. Serge took in her tight smile. A smile she knew didn't reach her eyes. She could feel how Cody's hand had tightened against her back. She could just imagine how tense his shoulders would look. How tight his jaw must be.

"They're yours, Serge." Her voice had an edge she couldn't help. "Cranberries with extra chocolate. Just the way you like them. I left the tin in the kitchen."

"You're the best, sis." His smile wasn't quite as wide this time.

"Have you finally set a date?" her father asked.

Oh god!

Here we go!

"Not now, Sampson," her mother chided. "We're still at the table." She dished up another slice of steak. Bless her mom. Always trying to keep the peace. She gave Demi a knowing smile. A kind smile. There was a world of sorrow in her mom's eyes as well.

"We're going for a walk after lunch." Cody sounded upbeat. "We're going to talk about it some more then."

"How much longer do you need to talk about it?" her dad asked, frustration etched in his voice. "Laird and I were discussing it a few days ago. This can't drag on for too much longer." Laird was Cody's father.

"I need more time," she said, scooping up more potato salad.

"You've had months," he snapped back.

"It's not long enough," she countered. They'd had this

conversation several times in the last few weeks. Too many times.

"I think we should at least look at setting a date," Cody said.

Demi felt panicky. He wasn't serious? The food suddenly felt like a rock inside her stomach. "Not yet," she managed to push out, hardly believing what she was hearing.

"It's been long enough." Her father's eyes narrowed.

Demi swallowed the lump in her throat. "Her body is barely cold in the ground and you want me—"

Her mother made a sobbing noise, her fork clanging as it hit the plate.

"I'm sorry," Demi choked on the words. "I shouldn't have said that." She rubbed a hand over her face. Her eyes stung.

Her father's eyes flashed with pain, but he quickly recovered. "Brie has been gone for over a year now. I understand how difficult this—"

"No, you don't. You have no idea. At least the two of you… " She stopped right there. Not wanting to hurt Cody.

Her father snorted. "I was the Alpha of the Vale Creek pack up until recently. I know full well. As does your mother. It isn't easy but it must be done." His eyes blazed. "The Alphas before us followed tradition, as did those before them. It is your turn now." His tone was hard and unyielding.

"Tradition," she said the word like it tasted bad. "It's outdated. It's unnecessary. We have a good standing with the bear pack. We—"

Cody pulled his hand away, shifting in his chair. Serge looked down at his plate, concentrating on eating. His whole frame radiated tension. Her mother folded her arms across her chest, her eyes misty.

"Only because of our age-old traditions. They are in place for a reason. There can only be one Alpha. Cody is the strongest bear male, hence him being the new Alpha. A continued amalgamation of the packs is required. That means—"

"I know what that means," she said under her breath. "I just wish there was another way."

"There is no other way. I know this is hard on you. None of us were to know that Brie... that... " His voice became strained. "We never prepared for this. *You* never prepared for this. It makes it harder on you. I understand that, but there is no other way. You have until the end of today to announce a date," her father said, pushing away his plate even though he wasn't quite done.

"But we—" she tried.

"That's final!" he all but growled. "Today! And the date needs to be this summer."

"The fall is only a few weeks from now." Her eyes pricked. Her throat felt like it was closing. "It's too soon. I'm not ready. I can't... we aren't—"

"Choose a day!" He slammed his hand on the table. Dishes shook and the salt shaker fell over. She could see he regretted it immediately. "Demi, you... " he spoke softly, carefully. His sudden change in tone cut her even more.

"Please excuse me from the table," she managed to get out. It felt like the walls were closing in.

"You can finish your lunch. We only... " her father began.

"Yes," her mother's voice was hitched, "you can go, sweetheart."

Demi nodded in her mother's direction, grateful for the reprieve. She couldn't trust herself to speak. She pushed her chair back and forced herself to walk calmly from the room, her eyes blurry with tears.

The door slammed shut behind her as she began to jog away. Her fur bristled beneath her skin. The need to shift hitting her... hard. It was easier in her animal form. Although she was still herself, her thoughts were less complicated. Things always seemed better... easier. Instincts took over. Different needs became more important. Things like running, jumping. Feeling the earth under her paws. The wind in her fur. The need to kill and to devour. Lately, there had been other needs too. Urges she refused to acknowledge. It wasn't like she could do anything about them.

Demi could hear him behind her. Could smell him as well. It was a scent she'd come to associate with Brie. She still did, dammit. Demi turned on her heel. "I'd like to be alone." Her voice was choked. Pain and anger clogging her throat. Tears stinging her eyes something fierce. "I want to run for a while. Clear my head"

"I thought you said you ran this morning?" Cody asked. Nope. He didn't ask. It wasn't a question but rather a statement.

She shrugged. *So what if she had?*

He lifted his brows. "It's important to be in our furs regularly, but—"

"I know exactly what you are going to say." She'd heard this before too. "Not too often though."

He shook his head. "You are half human as well you know. Spend too much time in your fur and you risk losing your humanity. You would risk losing you." He pointed at her.

"Is that so bad?" she mumbled.

"You're going to be the Alpha female of two packs, Demi. Yes, it would be bad. You can't give in to your wolf's demands."

"I can't believe you're not still fighting this, Cody. I can't believe you would do this to Brie. It's so wrong. You know that, don't you?"

His jaw worked. His eyes blazed with both anger and pain. Then they softened. "Your sister meant everything to me. The fact of the matter is… " He pulled in a breath. "I hate to even say it."

"Then don't!" she practically yelled.

"I have to though. I have to say it because it's the truth. Your sister… she's gone. She isn't coming back. We have to do this for the good of the people. For our families. For the Vale Creek pack's future." He cupped her cheek. "I'm beginning to think we *could* make this work."

She was too flabbergasted to say anything. She didn't even pull back. Her mouth would have dropped if it weren't for his hand on her jaw.

"I can see her in you… or you in her. I don't know which is more accurate." He smiled. "You have her eyes, you know? And very similar mannerisms. Your smile is— "

"Don't!" She pulled away, breaking the contact. "Don't you dare." She pointed a finger at him.

"Let's give it a chance." He was animated. "Let's try. Kiss me."

"No damned way." She shook her head, feeling panic well inside her. "How can you say something like that? How can you say any of it? You don't want me, Cody. You never did. You want Brie and I don't blame you. I refuse to live in her shadow though. To have you see her every time you look at me." It wasn't about that though. "I see you as a brother…

kiss you? Forget about it. We agreed that we would find a way out of this. You said once you were Alpha that you'd sort it out. Well, you've been Alpha for three weeks now. You've gone and done a one-eighty on me. What has changed?"

He made a groaning noise and ran his hand through his hair. "Nothing! Although that's not entirely true. I guess I've come to realize that... " He pushed out a breath, locking eyes with her. "I have feelings for you."

The ground fell out from under her. At least, that's how it felt. Demi staggered backwards two steps. "What?" She felt her blood run cold. "No way. You're trying to replace my sister with the next best thing."

Hurt blossomed in his eyes. "That's not true."

"Isn't it?" If she was honest with herself, she'd seen it change... the way he looked at her. She'd caught desperation in his stare as well. Cody was trying to use her to replace her dead sister. She was sure of it. It made this whole thing infinitely worse.

"I do see her, but I see *you* too. We need to try." He took a step towards her. "We have to make this work. Don't you see that?"

"I can't believe you're saying this." She shook her head. "No! There's no point in trying. I can't." *Did that make her selfish?* The thought of letting Cody touch her, kiss her... *Arghh! No!* "I can't do that to Brie."

"Brie is gone." He spoke softly and carefully, obviously sensing how spooked she was. "We are still here. Please." All at once, she could hear that manic laughter from her dream. She realized it wasn't real, and yet she could still hear it. Clear as a bell. She had to get away from Cody. Away from there.

She felt her fur sprout. Her snout extended and her jaw

cracked. "Never!" she managed to growl as she completed her change. Her clothing falling off her in a tattered, shredded mess. Then she was running and running and running. Feeling freer by the second. All her worries floated away.

CHAPTER 3

The clearing was very busy. Noisy too. But he had promised his brother he would attend. That he would stick around and join in the celebrations, and so here he was.

He took a plate and headed for the table. The scents coming off the various dishes were amazing. They made his mouth water. So the whole afternoon wasn't going to be a complete waste. He was going to grab himself a plate and then find a quiet spot to observe the activities. Hopefully, Mountain wouldn't stay too long. His brother had to be keen to spend time with his new mate. He—

Obsidian was concentrating so much on the food, he only realized someone was next to him after he bashed into them. Hard. The plate the other person had been holding, landed on the floor, breaking, food scattered across the floor.

By fucking scale, it was a mess!

"Hey!" the male growled. "Careful where—" He stopped speaking as soon as their eyes locked.

Great! It was Clay. Obsidian grunted what he hoped

sounded like an apology.

"You really should spend more time in your skin. More time with people in general. You're becoming more and more socially inept." Clay rolled his eyes. "You really do like living up to your name, Savage." He smiled as he said it.

"Don't!" Obsidian warned. He had said he was sorry. What more did the male want?

Then Clay took a step back and whistled low. "Wow, look at you." Although to anyone watching it would seem he was giving Obsidian a positive appraisal, he knew better. "Wearing clothes for a change I see." He looked down at Obsidian's pants. "I have to say… " he rubbed his chin, "I'm not sure I like the look. Too civilized for a male like you. Nice try though, Savage." He smirked.

Obsidian grit his teeth. He tried to ignore the male, concentrated on the table of food and on dishing up instead.

"So, you're not going to clean up the mess you made?" Clay went on. "Fucking typical!"

Obsidian turned his head to the male who was still smirking. Normally Clay wasn't quite so openly hostile towards him. He must have known that Obsidian wouldn't want to cause a scene at his brother's mating ceremony. That he was relatively safe. Right there and right then.

Obsidian held his own plate out to Clay who took it. The smirk quickly turned to a frown. Obsidian could see that Clay was preparing to say something. Obsidian abruptly turned and walked out, before he did something he would regret, like ruin his brother's celebration. He'd also hate to get blood all over the pants he was wearing and prove yet again, that he was indeed savage. That the nickname he had been given many years ago during one of the training sessions was apt.

Fuck that!

He was learning to control his strength. To control his beast. No, that wasn't entirely true. He had learned how to embrace his dragon side. To revel in his scales. Not something a male like Clay would understand. The male was a wet, simpering idiot, a sap.

Obsidian pulled his pants from his body, dropping the garment on the dusty earth, before stepping over them. He shifted in less than a second and took to the skies. Freedom. Quiet. Calm. Clarity of thought. He spread his wings and flapped harder, finding himself returning to the valley. Hoping to catch a glimpse of her.

Why though? He couldn't say.

Why he felt excitement when he caught sight of her, he couldn't say either, since this had nothing to do with attraction. Maybe it was recognizing another being fully exhilarated in their animal form that had him so intrigued. A flash of fur caught his eye and he realized she was there. She disappeared behind a rocky outcrop. *Must be in that thicket of trees.*

Obsidian beat his wings faster. *Where was she?* His eyes strained, trying to catch sight of her. She moved fast but she couldn't have gotten far. *Where was she?*

Hunt.

The forest was thick in these parts, sometimes giving way to open sections and the odd field. *There!* He caught sight of her body as she moved between the trees. He liked to watch her. Loved to watch her muscles move beneath her fur. How her body stretched out as she ran. Lithe and streamlined, yet powerful. He felt another tug inside him. The urge to hunt being brought straight to the fore. It wasn't quite the same feeling he normally got when on the chase. This was slightly different somehow. He couldn't put his claw on it. He usually felt this way when an animal was fleeing, yet she wasn't running *from* anything. She didn't even know he was there. The scent of fear also incensed him, and she didn't smell fearful at all. He caught her musky wolf scent; there were also smells of female mixed in there. Sweet and delicate. His mouth watered even though he wasn't hungry.

Hunt.

The desire to chase her brought him in closer. There was this voice inside him that told him to leave. It was his voice of reason. The rational side of him. His human side. He ignored it.

Hunt.

Obsidian glided in closer still. Moving silently. He could see her better now. Her coat was inky black. It glinted in the sun as she moved, her paws digging into the ground. Her breath came in short pants. Her eyes were big and dark and very beautiful.

Hunt.

Hunt.

The need grew in him. Only, he didn't want to tear at her flesh and to taste her hot blood as it pumped from her body. If he had been in his skin, he would have frowned right then. Why this compulsion to hunt if he wasn't going to kill? The question left him as soon as it entered his mind.

Hunt.

The wolf stopped so suddenly, he had to silently backtrack, using small flaps of his wings. *What was she doing?* She just seemed to be standing there in the clearing. Her chest heaved. Her breathing still shallow and fast. She stood like that for what felt like a long time. Her breathing slowly easing.

Then she was shifting, folding in on herself. All that inky fur gave way to skin. Smooth, soft, sun-kissed. Her hair was long and black as night. It looked thick and lush.

Obsidian had always preferred the she-dragons in their scales. He preferred fangs to teeth and scales to skin. He loved their long, delicate wings and barbed tails.

The female stood up, drawing his attention back to her. Her body was lithe and toned, only, there was a softness there that hadn't been present in her animal form. Like how her hips flared slightly. Her breasts were rounded and plump too. Not overly so, just big enough that they would feel good in his hands and bounce during a good rut. He held back a growl as his dick began to harden.

Hunt!

Now!

He ignored his reaction to her. Noting how her rump was nicely rounded as well. His cock twitched. The female was a perfect mix of strength and grace. Her hair looked silky soft… her lips were plump and—He realized too late how close he had gotten to her. He'd been so utterly enthralled by the creature before him, he'd allowed himself to drift closer and closer, until—

She sucked in a breath and turned, those dark eyes wide. They widened further as they landed on him, a stunned gasp leaving her mouth. Then she turned on her heel and ran. The wrong thing to do. His instincts took hold.

Hunt!

Hunt!

Hunt!

Although Obsidian gave chase, he didn't try as hard as his impulse was pushing him. He could have had her in his gasp already if he'd given in to his baser needs. She was fast in her human form, slowing down as she began to shift. What would he do with her if he caught her? He didn't understand his reaction to her. He'd never become aroused by another species before. Not even by the unmated, sweet-scenting humans who were on their territory from time to time. Yet, here he was hunting a wolf. Not just that, he was fully aroused and ready to rut. It made no sense. Maybe it was confusion after going without fucking for so long. Maybe that had sparked this raging need. He didn't actually plan on rutting her though. Even his animal side cringed at the thought. *What, then?*

Eat her? His mouth watered some more and yet the need for blood was still absent.

Talk to her? Laughable. Obsidian had less and less to say of late. This creature was not even his species. She turned back to him as she ran. Her eyes even wider… terror flared in their depths when she realized how close he was. It only succeeded in further incensing him. Obsidian surged forward, stretching out a claw, wanting to… what? Touch her? Grab her?

The female tripped over a root, mid-shift. He tried to reach for her. To stop her from falling, but he wasn't quite close enough. His claw caught the side of her arm as she fell.

With a yelp that sounded more animal than human, she face-planted in the dirt. She fell hard. He heard a muffled noise… sounding like a sob and then she was quiet. Her limbs had lengthened slightly and there was a light fur on her back and arms. It receded before his eyes. A sure sign that she was unconscious. Her legs returned to human length. Back to beautiful olive skin encasing toned muscle. Since when did he find skin so beautiful? He always preferred scales.

Obsidian sniffed at the female, scenting blood. His dick throbbed even more. He looked down at her plump rear. Could scent her pussy nestled between her legs. The need to rut hit him hard. It didn't matter that the female was injured. That she was even unconscious. He wanted her and he wanted her right then. His arms shook with the need to lift her ass up and to bury himself inside her.

He growled loudly, recoiling back, only then realizing that he was still in his dragon form. He could kill her if he rutted her in this state. Obsidian tried to breathe through his mouth. He tried to... calm the fuck down. He couldn't do this. It would be wrong. He wasn't an animal. Not entirely. He needed to...

Take!

Rut!

He moved a step towards her, clenching his jaw. He needed to do something to bring himself back to his senses but couldn't think of what that thing was. He could only scent her. He could only think of the tight pink folds he would find if he parted her thighs. He squeezed his eyes shut and roared, feeling angry. He couldn't have her.

Want!

Need!

Take!

His beast rode him hard. His cock throbbed. He grit his teeth, snarling in frustration. *No! No!* He would hurt her. Obsidian forced himself to smell her blood instead of her sex. To think of how fragile she was. Soft and delicate. Easily broken. *Must protect! Must… rut!*

Take!

Have!

Need!

He snarled so loudly that the earth shook.

CHAPTER 4

She tried to open her eyes but couldn't. Her head pounded.

What had—?

Her mouth hurt. Her… she groaned as she lifted her head, feeling blood gush from her nose, which felt like it might just be broken. It throbbed like mad. *Great!*

That's when she heard him snarl. He was right behind her. The beast. The one who had been stalking her. Holy hell but she'd never seen eyes like that. So focused on her. She didn't like what she read in them. Demi turned, slowly. Ever so slowly. He was a huge son of a bitch. Easily three or four times her size when in wolf form and she wasn't in her animal form right then.

His lip curled from his teeth in a silent snarl. By fur but those teeth were long and sharp. There were plenty of them. His scales gleamed and his tail whipped from side to side in an agitated fashion. She was dead. He was going to kill her. His eyes were filled with rage. He—

That's when she saw it… his… his… dragon-cock. It was

massive. Almost like a fifth limb. It jutted from between his hind legs. It seemed to be pointed at her. Why was it hard like that? Only one answer came to mind. By all the gods, if he tried anything, he would tear her in half. It would be the end of her. That was for sure.

Demi narrowed her eyes. If she just lay there, one way or the other, she would be dead. She pulled in a deep breath. *Here goes nothing.* Demi shifted. It took two seconds and for that precious moment, she was vulnerable. She half expected him to pounce right then but he didn't. It was puzzling. Not shifting hadn't been an option since she needed to fight him. Maybe she'd get lucky and find a weakness.

He snarled, his muscles bunching, making him seem even bigger. *Weakness? Like hell!* This dragon didn't have any weaknesses that she could see. Demi had to try though. There was no other option.

She crouched, her fur bristling. Should she attempt to outrun him? She'd bet anything she was faster, just by looking at his sheer bulk. The problem were those blasted wings. Running wasn't an option. He'd catch her in half a second flat. She snarled as she attacked him, raking her claws across his chest before darting away.

The dragon snarled in anger, smoke billowed from his nose. *Shit!* He could burn her to a crisp. She hadn't thought about that. Demi glanced back between his legs, that massive cock twitched. Burning would be better than being rammed to death with that thing. If rutting her was even his intention. She wasn't sure. So far, he hadn't made a move. Maybe looking aroused like that was normal for a dragon. It didn't seem right though. Why was he just standing there? The look in his eyes scared the shit out of her. Demi circled a little to the right and sprang back at him, expecting him to make a grab for her. Or to hit her away, something. He didn't though. *Was he that slow?* Big, cumbersome and sluggish? It didn't seem right, but she'd take it. Anything to get the edge. This time she went for his right shoulder and took her time, digging her claws in as far as they would go. He snarled as she pulled back. By then he had several cuts on his chest. The fresh one on his right shoulder dripped blood.

Good!

Go away! She snarled at him. He'd understand her. *Leave me alone!* It was universal.

Demi only hoped he would leave soon. Why was he just standing there? What was going through his mind? What did he want?

She prowled, just outside of his immediate reach, keeping her eyes on him, trying to decide on her next move. He roared as she came at him again. It was loud and terrifying. His whole body vibrated. The sound scared her enough to keep her from doing too much damage. Her paws glanced off him, barely leaving a scratch. Demi jumped away. She was already panting. The long run had taken it out of her. She couldn't carry on like this indefinitely.

The dragon snarled, finally making his move and holy crap but he was quick. The creature was like liquid lighting, and on her in a second. He knocked her over, crouching over her, so that he had her pinned with his big body. Heat radiated off of him.

Demi fought to free herself, she was horrified to find that she was whining, like she'd lost already.

No!

Screw that!

A growl found its way out of her as she scratched and clawed at his chest. He leaned in, his face directly over hers.

His snout almost touching hers. His lips curled back. His eyes… by fur but they terrified her. Slitted, like a reptile. She couldn't see much human in them. Normally shifters kept their humanity, even in animal form. Not this dragon. All she saw was feral rage. Maybe he would kill her after all.

She whined again, softer this time. There was no way she was winning this fight on strength. Not with that jaw poised above her. Or those claws on either side of her. Long and sharp. It wasn't going to happen. She needed to appeal to his human side. The male side of him had to be in there somewhere. Buried deep and perhaps even unreachable.

No, that wasn't true. He'd been holding back. He was still holding back. He had her. He could kill her or worse, and yet, he didn't do anything. She didn't know what to make of him.

Demi had to force herself to shift. It was no easy feat. Her instincts compelled her to stay in her fur. She was stronger as an animal than a human. Stronger, faster and more difficult to kill. It was ultimately safer, but she couldn't communicate that way. Not really. She needed to make herself vulnerable and hopefully he would leave her be.

His eyes stayed on hers. Hard and cold. She forced herself to look away. She would never be able to shift under such scrutiny. Summoning all her strength, Demi shifted. It took a few seconds longer than normal. Seconds that felt more like minutes. She'd never felt more vulnerable in her whole life. Never more terrified than in that moment.

"Please," she whispered, as soon as she was in her human form. "Please don't hurt me," she pleaded.

His eyes narrowed and he growled. She could feel the vibration run through her body.

"What do you want? My name is Demi. My family will be

searching for me." Not true. She was known to disappear for hours at a time, sometimes even for a whole day. That meant that she was completely at his mercy.

Demi realized she was panting, but couldn't stop, not with the amount of adrenaline coursing through her system. The need to shift back was almost overwhelming but she managed to suppress it. There was a flash of something in his eyes as he leaned in to sniff her. Something human? It was too quick to tell.

Demi whimpered, trying hard to stay still. The dragon sniffed some more. It could only mean one of two things, he was going to kill and eat her, or he wanted to rut her. She very quickly got her answer. The beast tilted its head back, arching away from her. He roared loudly, more smoke billowing. This was it. She was dead. Yet, instead of ripping her to shreds, she heard the first telltale cracking noise as he began to shift. He didn't plan on killing her then, or he would have done so. That left the other... *Stay calm, Demi! Stay calm!* She didn't know that for sure.

He growled and snarled as his features began to shift, scales receding. His jaw pulled in and then lengthened. The scales popped back out. He snarled again, sounding frustrated and angry.

This beast was so far gone that he couldn't even shift. He arched his back again, more smoke billowed. His wings were only half the length they had been. They flapped aimlessly as he tried to shift. His body was misshapen. Somewhere in-between. It had to hurt.

This was her chance.

Maybe her only chance.

Demi squirmed her way out from under him and flipped herself over onto all fours. She began to crawl, feeling fur sprout. She fell forward as a weight settled on her. His weight. His breath was in her ear and against the crook of her neck. His body was crouched over her. Pushing down. A hand splayed on her belly holding her in place. She felt both skin and scale. Hands and talons. Not long enough to pierce but certainly long enough to feel. He was still somewhere mid-shift, but then so was she.

"Don't move," he growled the words. They sounded deep, resonating and guttural.

She squirmed, wanting so badly to lash out. To run.

Her body must have tensed, poised itself to do just that because he said, "Don't!" His hand tightening on her belly.

She could feel his cock. Hard and ready, pressed up tightly against her ass. *No! No! No!*

"I won't… " The rest came out sounding like more of a growl than words.

Demi was gulping down air, trying not to panic. She squeezed her eyes shut, trying to stop herself from whining. It would only incense him. She needed to stay completely still, completely quiet and remain submissive, otherwise, she was dead.

"… won't… hurt… " more growling. He ground his teeth, sounding frustrated. He was trying to tell her that he wasn't going to hurt her. If that was true, why was he holding her down like this?

She wanted to believe him but was struggling to do so. Then again, he hadn't hurt her. Not yet. Not intentionally. The fall had been her own clumsiness. Her face already felt mostly healed. He hadn't actually touched her. Most of the blood was his. Maybe he meant it. "O-okay." Her voice was still a touch panicked. Her breathing still labored. "Let me go," she tried.

"Can't." The word sounded more human. Now that she thought about it, she could feel more skin instead of scales. His hand was no longer tipped with claws. It felt like any other hand. His dick, however, was just as hard. Still pressed firmly against her. Still huge.

"W-why… " she was almost too afraid to ask, "n-not?"

"Lose… " His voice was still deep. His chest vibrated against her back. "Control." It was like he had to concentrate to say each word.

His chest heaved. His breathing sounded labored. His cock still throbbed against her.

She squeezed her eyes shut, trying hard to calm down. "Lose control how?" She swallowed. "You'll hurt me? Kill me? Oh god!" she whined, her wolf practically begging to be let out. She needed to shut the hell up! To stop showing weakness.

"Don't run."

She pulled in a deep breath and nodded once.

"Don't fight."

"I said I wouldn't," she snapped back at him. "My instincts are telling me to do both though."

"My…" he growled, "instincts… hunt… want… hunt… you."

"You have me."

He kept his arm clutched around her. They stayed that way for a good minute. The seconds ticking by slowly… ever so slowly. It was killing her.

"Are you starting to feel better yet?" It seemed to be working. His muscles had relaxed some.

He made a low growling noise. It sort of sounded like an affirmation. Then he loosened his hold on her belly. "Don't… run," he warned again.

"I said I wouldn't." Her voice was much less panicked. "You could have hurt me already, but you haven't. I'd wager that you have far more control than you think." She prayed it was true.

"Not… much."

Shit! "Okay. I'll stay still. I won't fight. Please, just calm down."

"Trying." His voice was laced with frustration.

It helped her to know that he was trying so hard. At the same time, it was more difficult to stay still without him holding her against himself. "My name is Demi."

Nothing. Just the throbbing of his cock against her ass.

"This is the part where you tell me your name."

"Obsidian."

Even his name had a scary ring about it. It was a strong name. "Obsidian."

He growled, sounding angry again. His hand tightened around her belly once more.

"Easy," she whispered. "You don't want to hurt me. We can get through this."

Again nothing. *Shit!*

"Can you let me turn over. I want to talk to you." Demi wanted to look into his eyes. He couldn't harm her as easily if he was looking into her eyes. "Please. I'll stay on my back. I won't move. I swear. We'll talk."

He loosened his hold, finally taking his hand away. "Don't like to talk." His voice was still incredibly gruff. It certainly didn't sound like he used it much.

"Why is that?" He still felt tense. His body poised for action.

She felt movement against her. It felt like he had just

shrugged. *Good!* It meant he was relaxing. "People talk a lot but, in the end, they say nothing. No one listens much either."

She thought back to her earlier discussion with her father. Demi recalled her conversation with Cody as well. "You're right about that." She slowly lowered herself to her stomach, feeling dirt and clumps of grass beneath her. Then she turned over, moving carefully and deliberately so as not to spook him.

The first thing she noticed were his eyes. They were a beautiful light chestnut color. They were soft now that the slitted pupils were gone. She saw intelligence. Looking up into them made her feel instantly calmer. There was still animal there but not like before. Not nearly. He wasn't going to hurt her. She was almost certain of it.

When she looked beyond his eyes, she realized how good-looking he was. It was pretty crazy of her to notice at a time like this, but there it was anyway. His dark hair was a bit shaggy and overgrown, which actually added to the appeal. His lips were full, for a male. His lashes were also long and dark, making his eyes quite beautiful. His jaw was very masculine, as was the stubble on his face. He was hands down the biggest male she had ever seen, which was nuts considering that her pack was made up of both wolf and bear shifters. Bears, Cody included, were massive both in their human and animal forms. They had nothing on Obsidian. Even Cody, the biggest of them all, had nothing on this male. His shoulders were broad. His arms and chest were well-muscled.

He was still in a crouching position above her. Now that she was flat on her back, there was a fair bit of space between them. She was sure to keep her eyes on his face though. Not wanting to give him any ideas. She was pretty sure he would still be sporting an erection. Something like that didn't just disappear.

His eyes narrowed on her and he cocked his head slightly. "You are sad."

Her first thought was a cocky one. *No shit! Of course I'm sad, I'm about to be eaten by a big, bad dragon.* A look of concern crossed his face and he gently, ever so softly touched her face with the tip of one finger. It was a ghost of a touch. Leaving her feeling like she might have imagined it.

"Yes." She gave the tiniest of nods. "I am." It scared her to realize just how sad she was. How the emotion churned in her. "Sad, lonely, depressed… I'm angry too."

"Mostly sad though." He nodded once. "I understand." Then his eyes drifted down, first to her mouth and then lower.

Demi swallowed thickly as his brow furrowed.

Shifters were not generally concerned too much with nudity but the way he was looking at her… well, it should have had her squirming or covering up. Instead, it felt like her skin tightened.

Obsidian looked confused. "Your skin," he shook his head, "it looks so soft." He touched the side of her arm. His eyes flicked back up to hers. "Very soft." He sounded in awe, looking back down. He touched her belly, his hand slowly moving up and up and—

She sucked in a breath when he cupped her breast. He squeezed, making her suck in another breath. His touch was leaning more towards exploratory than sexual and yet… gooseflesh broke out on her arms. Was she so attention-starved that she was enjoying this? She had missed having a connection with another person. She'd missed rutting. She was a shifter after all. Her sex drive was high. Over a year of abstinence suddenly felt like a really long time.

She wasn't actually attracted to this male? Like that? Now? At a time like this? Surely not. It didn't seem—She groaned when he raked a thumb over her nipple. Demi felt it between her legs. Her clit did this zinging thing. Her belly clenched. Her toes even curled. Shifters were not designed to go without sex. She felt that so acutely right then, it was scary. Okay, well maybe she was attracted to the dragon.

He looked down, focusing on her... pussy. Demi pushed her legs together, almost groaning at how she felt there. How achy. How—He sniffed. *Shit!* She was turned on. Her wolf was yipping and whining. It wanted her to turn over, to lift her ass. Her eyes drifted down. His thighs were powerful. His hips narrow. By freaking fur but his cock was massive, a bead of pre-cum amassing on his tip. She licked her lips.

"Female," a throaty growl she felt between her legs. She realized his hand was back on the ground next to her. He was no longer touching her. There was a feral look in his eyes. It was desire. Wild, unabashed need... and for her. Demi had never seen this level of raw desire before. His forehead was creased in a deep frown. His jaw was set.

Her nipples were tight nubs. Her pussy felt wet. Her breathing was ragged, her heart raced.

His lip pulled back in a silent snarl and his muscles bunched. Demi put a hand on his chest. His skin was hot, a few degrees higher than hers. He closed his eyes, seeming to relish the contact. She leaned up, brushing her lips over his, marveling at how soft they were.

He growled low and deep. "Fuck." He wasn't cussing. Obsidian was making a statement.

He growled again. It was a sound that should terrify her.

She should be running right about then. The words *'What the hell am I doing?'* should have been clanging through her brain. Shrill alarm bells should have been going off. None of that was happening though. Not when his breathing turned ragged as well. Not when he clasped a hand around her thigh. Not when he nudged her legs open. Not when he settled himself between her parted thighs.

All she felt was need.

Aching want.

His eyes stayed on hers as he hooked his arms around the backs of her legs, her pelvis tilting up. He moved slowly, even though she could feel his hands shaking. His teeth were clenched tight. He put his cock against her opening. It was like he was counting to three with each step. Like he was giving her time to object. It was that, or he was trying to keep himself calm by pausing. She yelled out as he pushed into her. Obsidian snarled as he pushed deeper.

He was big and she hadn't done this in forever, so it stung. He didn't move. Three whole seconds in suspension. She realized that her eyes were closed tight. Obsidian pulled back before thrusting into her, going deeper this time. It hurt but she could feel the pleasure there too somewhere. Again, he waited before pulling back and thrusting. Three seconds of sting and then a thrust of pain. The pain slowly giving way to pleasure, the sting slowly evolving into need… for more.

She yelled when he bottomed out… as he touched her there. Deep. He used the three seconds to adjust her position, lifting her legs higher on his back. Then he all out fucked her, using hard, punchy thrusts. The pain was gone. In its place, blinding pleasure. One hand held his shoulder, while the other gripped his meaty ass. She could feel his muscles bunch and release beneath his skin as her fingers dug in. Could feel the slick sweat coating his skin. Obsidian wasn't quiet about it either. He snarled and growled and grunted. He arched back, eyes closed, a look of ecstasy on his handsome face. Then he opened his eyes. They were beautiful, hazy with desire. They seemed to look right into her. He slowed a little for a few thrusts. She watched his pupils change shape, slowly turning slitted. Then his thrusts increased in tempo. Harder. Deeper.

She gave a startled cry as her orgasm hit her. Demi felt it everywhere and all at once. Her back bowed. The earth digging into her back... not that she could feel it right then. Her toes curled. She felt him poise for a beat... maybe two, then he jerked into her and roared. The sound deafening and yet exhilarating all the same. His neck muscles roped, and he got a shocked look, like he couldn't quite believe it was happening. Pleasure still rippled through her when Obsidian pulled out. He flipped her over, her knees giving in. His hand was back on her belly as he hoisted her up, his cock sliding back into her pussy, taking her deep.

The new angle felt good. He pulled her ass up a little higher and she whimpered, feeling another release building inside her. So soon. Her eyes widened up. Her mouth was wide open as she gasped for air. Then his finger was on her clit. *Rub, rub, rub* and she was clutching at the earth as a second orgasm rushed through her. Demi's mouth fell open even more, then she groaned deep, clenching her teeth.

Obsidian jerked against her, his hips hitting against her ass. Her breasts jerking forward. He groaned as well, the sound filled with such pleasure. He slowed down. His cock still moving in and out of her, his seed running down her inner thighs. His grunts and her ragged pants filled the clearing. He finally stopped moving, letting his head rest on her back. His chest heaved against her. His dick throbbed inside her, still hard. She struggled to get enough air in.

The dragon had just given her the best sex of her life. It had been hard. More animal than human, even though they were both in their skins, but it had been the best. She didn't know this male at all and yet, here she was, on her knees, his cock deep inside her, her body vibrating from the sheer pleasure.

No future. No past. Just right then. Funny how she'd known Cody for years and yet the thought of the male anywhere near her made her feel ill.

Oh crap!

Hell!

Cody.

Her life.

Her pack. Holy shit! What had she just done?

"You okay?" he asked, pulling out of her. Obsidian sat back. She fell onto her elbows as he pulled away. The horror of how this was going to affect not just her, but others, descended on her. Demi couldn't help it. It was like the gates to her emotions had just been opened, she burst into tears. The reality of her life finally sunk in.

CHAPTER 5

Obsidian felt extreme euphoria as his blood rushed through his veins. His whole body vibrated, still coming down from a high.

He'd just had the best rut of his entire life, so it was to be expected. It even beat out his first rut – and by a mile. He'd never felt a pussy quite so tight or so wet. Never had a female so vocal or receptive. Her eyes were beautiful. So dark. So lovely. Just like every part of her. He loved how hazy they became as he fucked her. He loved how she chewed on her lip and then clenched her jaw just before she had come. He loved how she felt on the end of his cock. He loved the beautiful golden color of her skin and how soft it felt. All of it shocked him. A wolf – and in her skin at that – should not be so attractive to him. He'd never taken a female on her back before, had never looked into her eyes while he rutted. He had enjoyed it far too much. Then again, it had been a very long time since he had rutted. *That had to be it.*

Obsidian was trying to decide whether to rut her again or whether to lick her slit until she creamed all over his face. He was still debating when she tensed up underneath him. She made this little noise that told him all was not well.

By scale but maybe he had hurt her. Or worse – he felt himself panic – what if she hadn't wanted this at all? Maybe she had given him mixed signals. Maybe she had felt so good he hadn't heard her say 'no.' Maybe he'd terrified her so badly that she hadn't been able to say 'no.'

That couldn't be though. *No fucking way!* He pulled back. "You okay?" he forced himself to say the words rather than to snarl them. "Hurt?" he growled. "Hurt you?" He moved until he was sitting, lifting her onto his lap. Obsidian smoothed the hair from her face.

The female was crying. Tears streamed down her cheeks. She was all out sobbing. Pausing to pull in deep breaths. She turned her head into his chest.

By scale, he didn't know what to do. Nothing like this had ever happened to him before. She had definitely come. Twice. And hard. Surely she had wanted the rutting? Surely he hadn't hurt her? "Demi," he said her name as he suddenly remembered what it was.

"I'm fine," she pushed out between sobs, but her shoulders only shook harder. Her cries of anguish grew louder.

"Please." He rubbed her back. "Tell me. You are not fine." He was at a total loss. "This is not fine."

"Hold me. Just hold me." She put an arm around his waist. She sobbed between hard breaths. "It's not you. Not…" He felt her shake her head. "I'm sorry."

Oh! Yes! It made sense to him then. It was the sadness he had seen in her eyes. She'd mentioned other emotions as well. Sadness was the main one though. He'd seen it, scented it, it was unmistakable. Obsidian had thought that he was sad. It wasn't just sorrow or depression he felt. Although he was angry a lot too. It sometimes got him into trouble. His biggest feeling was that of loneliness. He suspected she might be suffering from the same.

Obsidian hooked an arm around her, pulling her in close. He cupped the back of her head in his hand. "I've got you," he whispered as she sobbed against his chest.

He held her like that for a long time. Her breathing finally slowed, as did her sobs. She fell asleep in his arms. Obsidian didn't move, although he suspected she wouldn't wake even if he did. He wasn't willing to take the risk. This female was completely spent.

He sat there until his back ached. Until his right butt cheek went completely numb. The sun finally set, the forest falling to shadows. The shadows gave way to night.

Only then did she stir in his arms. Demi lifted her head with a startled intake of breath. Her eyes were hazy. "Where... what?" Her voice was hoarse with sleep. She glanced his way, her eyes widening. She scrubbed a hand over her face. "Oh shit!" she announced, trying to get off his lap. "It's dark," her voice sounded panicked, "I need to get home. I can't believe I slept... so long and," she forced out a breath, "so deeply." She tried to stand up a second time.

Obsidian held onto her. "Wait." He gulped. He'd never been good with words. "Are you... okay?"

She looked sheepish, looking down and then back up at him. "I'm fine." She smiled, but it didn't reach her eyes. He could scent fear as well, which worried him.

Obsidian narrowed his eyes. "Why are you afraid?"

"I'm not... I'm..." She stopped. "I'm going to be in trouble when I get back... that's all. I'm fine though. I haven't slept like that in a long time." Her eyes softened. "I guess I, I needed it. All of it." She leaned in and kissed him. Touching her lips to his for half a second.

Obsidian was too startled to do anything. He had never kissed anyone before. This was the second time she had done it to him, and he found he liked it.

"Thank you," she said, drawing his attention to her.

"Still sad." He cupped her cheek, seeing the emotion in her eyes. Dark and lovely but filled with such sorrow that it made his own chest tighten, even though he didn't know this wolf. He somehow felt connected to her now, after they'd rutted, which was idiotic. It was just fucking. Nothing more or less. Two people needing release and finding it with one another. She did intrigue him though. He wouldn't have been there otherwise.

She bit down on her lower lip and shrugged. Like her sorrow was just one of those things. "I'll be fine."

"You sure? Not good at talking but I'm a good listener." His voice was sharp and jagged from disuse. Like he'd swallowed barbed thorns. It was good to speak again though. Now that he had a reason to do so.

This time he let her get up. She was gorgeous under the moonlight. All long limbs. She smiled. "Listening… that's not all you're good at."

Obsidian smiled back. He felt his cheeks heat, feeling like a whelp again.

"I should get going." She toed the sand. It didn't matter what she said. He had learned to look past words, he could see that she didn't really want to leave.

"But you don't want to." He stood up as well, stretching out his aching muscles.

She shook her head. "What? Get back to reality? Not at all, but I have to."

"I want to rut you again."

She laughed. "Straight to the point."

"Yes." Thankfully she seemed to like that about him. "I think you would feel better if—" *What was that?* His senses twitched. Obsidian lifted his chin, he sniffed the air.

"What is it?" She frowned.

"Something is approaching."

"I can't hear anything." She looked worried, her eyes moving upwards and then from left to right. "Are you sure?" she whispered.

"Yes." He nodded. "More than one body, and with purpose. Not human. Still far away but moving fast." Obsidian frowned. "Wolves and something bigger… heavy…" He sniffed the air, trying to lock down on the scent.

"A bear."

"Yes… that's it. It's a bear. Wolves and bears… a strange combination." He frowned.

"Shit!" Her eyes clouded with fear. "It's probably Cody. It's night time already. I don't normally stay out this late. We had a fight… he might have checked up on me and found me gone." Her eyes were wide. The female dropped down into a crouch, her eyes narrowing and her back arching slightly. She whined once, looking like she might shift at any second.

He could scent adrenaline. Why was she reacting like this? Who was this male? They couldn't be together, since he hadn't scented anyone on her. Demi was sad and fearful for a reason though. He didn't like it. Not one bit.

"Go." She moved back to her full height and pushed at him. "You shouldn't be here when they arrive," she added, starting to look panicked. "I don't want any trouble." She looked in the direction they were coming from. "We shouldn't have rutted."

Obsidian shook his head. "You're afraid. I'm not leaving. I will wait until this Cody gets here. I will make sure you are safe."

"I *am* safe," she insisted, but he wasn't buying it. Her body's reaction told him "Please, I'm fine. Just go," she whispered, pushing at his chest again. "I don't want any trouble for you. I'm in a boatload as it is." More fear wafted from her. More adrenaline. Her eyes flashed to the sound of the approaching males and then back to him.

"Is someone hurting you?" he growled, trying to keep his voice low.

"It's not what you think," she whispered.

"Why are you so worried?" he insisted. Warning bells clanged inside his mind.

"It doesn't concern you!" she snapped, lifting her chin in defiance. "Thank you for the rut. I enjoyed myself. Even though you shouldn't have, thank you for letting me sleep for so long." Her whole demeanor softened. "I need to get back to my life now. It was nice just to forget about everything for a little while, but… it's over now. You need to go… if they find you here with me after what just happened… you'll be hurt. They may even kill you."

Fear.

Adrenaline.

The sorrow in her eyes.

Obsidian didn't give a shit about himself. He was sure he could take a few shifters easily. He was worried about Demi. Were these others going to hurt her? They were getting closer now. So close that she could hear them now too. Her eyes widened, her heart went nuts.

Fuck it!

Obsidian partially shifted. It took him less than a second. It was a little trick he had learned. He'd have the strength and speed of a dragon without the size and massive wingspan. He picked the female up and began to run through the dense forest.

What the hell was he doing?

Obsidian ran so fast her eyes stung. "No!" she yelled, looking in the direction they had just left. Her pack was hot on their heels. She could just make out the sounds of their padded footfalls, their yips and growls as her scent must have grown stronger. It would be Cody, her father, her brother maybe. There might even be one or two members of the wolf pack.

She cringed. They would be able to scent what she had done. Shame burned inside her. It quickly gave way to anger. *Screw it.* She had never agreed to mating Cody. Why were they even there looking for her? After their conversation, Cody must have assumed that she had run away. Demi had been tempted and still was. They entered a sparse section of the forest.

Before she could think about it anymore, she heard more cracking. Demi felt more scales erupt from the skin beneath her fingers. Then he was taking to the air through a gap in the canopy, flying so swiftly her eyes watered and her vision briefly faded black. Flickering a few times before coming back into focus. The ground pulling away so rapidly it made her feel nauseous.

Why was he doing this?

Why not just leave like she had asked?

Surely, he didn't think there was something between them after one rut? It had been good, but it didn't change things for her. It hadn't meant anything.

They flew for five or ten minutes, the ground a blur below them. For such a big male, he was quick, his wings silent. They landed next to a river. It flowed fast, the water surging and churning.

She watched open-mouthed as Obsidian, still in dragon form, waded into the water. The male was strong. Water moving at that speed, currents like those, would have taken most who dared try that. She inhaled and headed to the bank herself. Demi drank deeply and then, wading to her knees, she washed as best she could. Even here, so close to the bank, the currents were fierce.

Demi walked back out and folded her arms, waiting for Obsidian. A minute later, he waded out as well, giving his big body a shake. Water droplets went flying. Then he walked over to where she was standing and growled.

"Why did you bring me here? My home is back there." She pointed in the direction they had just left.

Obsidian made a growling, grunting noise.

"I'm afraid I don't speak dragon. You need to take me back." She tried to keep her voice even. She might not know the male, but she believed him to be a good man. Big and powerful but harmless.

Obsidian shook his great head. He growled low. Then he started shifting. The process long and laborious. Not as bad as before though.

"Wow," she said, as he finally stood before her in his skin. "That looked… difficult. Possibly even painful."

"I spend too much time…" he cleared his throat, his

voice thick, deep and corded, "in my scales."

"I'm being told the same more and more often of late. About my fur, that is." She smiled. "Although I'll bet I'm not half as bad as you. Why did you bring me here?"

"You're sad and afraid. The approach of others was making you worse. I couldn't leave you there." He clenched and unclenched his fists. "Are you in trouble?"

"No." She shook her head. It felt so good to have someone actually care. To actually see her. Hear her, even though she hadn't said anything. "My sister died," her voice choked up.

"I'm sorry." He moved towards her, clutching a hand around her elbow. The gesture was friendly and warm. It was gentle, as was the concern in his eyes.

"A freak accident. A car accident if you would believe it?" She felt her eyes well with tears. "Her soon-to-be mate was driving." She blinked a couple of times. "They went over a cliff. The car rolled and ended up wrapped around a tree. Her... her..." She swallowed. "It was bad," she finally said, shaking her head. Trying not to recall the state her older sister was in when they had pulled her from the wreckage.

"Why do I get the feeling this gets worse?" Obsidian squeezed her upper arm.

"Because it does." She clutched her hands together in front of her. "Brie died a little over a year ago. She was my older sister. The promised Alpha of the Vale Creek wolf pack. Cody is the promised Alpha of the bear pack, who resides in the same territory. The two packs used to be at war. For many years there was blood shed over who had control of the two packs, since neither pack would leave. Both felt they had a right to be there. The elders always say that you had to live during that time to truly understand."

"I understand." Obsidian nodded. "We are four different dragon species… we have lived through terrible wars amongst our own. There are still tensions."

"I am told that there are still tensions amongst the two packs as well. None that I can see but I am told they are there, and that war could break out at any time. That is why we have an agreement in place with the bears. There is an event that takes place every forty years that ensures a wolf and a bear mate. Not just any, but the strongest of each species. We hold a tournament for the children of the village. The winning male and female are called The Promised. They must be of the opposite sex. Bears and wolves take turns on who the male Alpha will be. One generation it is the bear and the next it is the wolves' turn. This because the male decides what the offspring will be. If the male is a bear, then the young will be bear-shifters. Same with the wolves."

He nodded. "It is the same for dragons."

"Everything is done to ensure fairness and that the peace is kept between our species."

"Interesting."

"There are runners-up. It is a hugely prestigious occasion. The winners are showered with praise." She widened her eyes for a moment. "Cody and Brie, my sister, won the event and became promised to one another as children. Brie was fourteen and Cody was fifteen. The future Alpha male and female. They were raised with the knowledge that they would mate one day."

"Forgive me, but that's… it's…" Obsidian was frowning.

"Weird?" she offered.

He nodded. "Very strange. At least, that it is still

enforced."

"It's tradition. It's normal. It's… how it is. Thankfully Cody and Brie were very much in love. They belonged together. They were a week away from their mating ceremony when…" Her lip quivered.

"The accident?"

"Yes." She nodded, clearing her throat and the lump that had lodged itself there. "The worst day of our lives. We were so close. She was my best friend. We spoke about everything. Her first kiss… how much she loved Cody, their mating… all of it. I missed her unbearably, I still do. That's why, when my father called me in for a meeting. When he told me what would be expected as next in line…" She paused for a moment, gathering her thoughts. "You see, I was the runner-up the day of the tournament. When Brie died, I became the promised female. The future Alpha female wolf."

She could see Obsidian processing the information. His eyes narrowed and his jaw tensed. "Don't tell me." He shook his head, letting her arm go. "They expect you to… to pick up where your sister left off?"

She nodded. "At first I outright refused. Then I begged and pleaded. Cody has always been in full agreement with me. He has hated the idea as much as I have."

"It's sick," Obsidian growled. "I'm sorry, but…"

"No, you're right. It *is* sick and yet, it's being forced on us. On me." She licked her lips. "Especially since Cody is on board with the whole thing all of a sudden. He changed his mind. I've noticed a change in him since he was ordained Alpha. He spoke to me today to convince me to go with it, to give him… us a chance. How can I be expected to mate my dead sister's lover? Her promised one? How? I've only ever seen him as a brother. I will never see him as more."

"That's why you are so sad?"

She nodded. "I'm sad because I lost my sister. Sad because of what is expected from me now that she is gone. Angry at the same time. I also feel guilty because I am letting my pack down. Refusing to mate Cody could bring on a war. I'm also lonely…" She laughed. "Hence what happened between us, I guess."

Obsidian had this look in his eyes that she couldn't interpret. He finally nodded once. "Okay," he said.

"Okay what?" She frowned.

"I will save you from this terrible tradition being forced upon you. I like you. I will mate you."

She looked at him for a few long seconds, waiting for him to laugh or, to say something else. Something that would make that statement make more sense. He didn't. Obsidian remained completely deadpan. His chestnut eyes staying firmly on her. Demi felt her jaw drop open.

"Why the shock? We are good… together."

She shook her head, sending her hair flying about her face. "We had decent sex… sure but… I mean… there is more to a relationship."

"Not really. I will provide for you in all ways. If you are already mated to me, they can't force you into anything."

"Let's just say I was to agree. It wouldn't solve anything. There could still be war between the wolves and the bears of Vale Creek and, as my father likes to say, it will be on me if that happens."

"It won't happen." He shook his head, looking deadly serious.

"How can you be so sure?"

"I will beat any who try to start shit."

She chuckled, believing him. "That sounds like a good plan."

"It's a perfect plan. I will make you happy… there will be plenty of screaming coming from our chamber. Not screams of anger," he quickly set the record straight.

She snorted out a laugh. "I figured that much. As tempted as I am, I'm going to have to decline." She took his hand, squeezing it once before letting go. "You are beyond sweet to offer."

His eyes dipped to her mouth, then to her neck. Her heart picked up speed, she was sure the pulse at the base of her neck must be jumping. "What?" she asked.

"I would like to try to convince you," he cleared his throat, "to change your mind about me. About us."

"How do you plan on doing that?"

He smiled for a second time since she had met him. By claw but it did things to her insides. These dimples – appeared one in each cheek. They softened his otherwise hard features. Making him even more handsome. "I would like to rut you again, for a start."

She folded her arms and barked out a laugh. "I'm sure you would."

"Only to show you how compatible we could be together."

"I think I might already have an inkling of that."

"No, you don't." He flashed her another half-smile. One she felt between her legs. "I'd hunt for you… build a shelter. We could… get to know one another." He cleared his throat again. "Sorry, I haven't talked this much in years."

"I'm honored."

"You should be," he stated. A fact. Not to sugarcoat anything. Not to be charming. Pure fact. "I want you, Demi." So darned serious. It was sexy on him.

"Believe it or not," she smiled up at him, "I'm tempted. Very tempted – which says a lot about my mental state. I can't though." She shook her head.

"You can."

"I really can't." She shook her head. "My family is worried about me. They will be able to scent… what happened between us. I'm sure that was them back there. Cody will be angry. He will see it as a slight, I am sure."

"It was four wolves and three bears."

"Shit! So many?" She pushed out a solid breath. She had been hopeful that her time with Obsidian could be kept under wraps. She didn't love Cody in that way, but he was a good male. She was going to hate seeing him hurt. Seeing the rumors spread around the pack. Nothing had been officially announced about the two of them, but everyone knew what the logical next step was. "They'll know what we did," she muttered, more to herself.

"What happened was perfectly natural. They will be able to scent that you don't want that male… Cody." He growled his name. "That you had a good time with me."

"The bears will see it as a slight. My father will see it as a betrayal. Cody…" She chewed on her lip for a second. "He might be hurt. He doesn't love me – I actually think he is trying to use me to replace Brie – but still… he would be upset by it."

"I'm glad it happened. I loved every second." His face grew pinched. "I'm not apologizing. Neither should you."

"I loved every second too." *Shit!* Now she was making it

out as if she wanted to undo the last few hours. It wasn't true though. Not even close.

"The thing I can't get out of my mind is your reaction when you knew they were coming. I see it as a cry for help. I am here to help you." He cupped her jaw.

"Thank you." She took his other hand, marveling at how big and warm it was. "I appreciate it."

"We're compatible. I think we could—"

"We are *not* meant to be, Obsidian. I'm sorry but that's the way it is." She wished things could be different. She wouldn't rush into a mating but there was something there. She liked this dragon. Was very attracted to him. It didn't mean she could forget her life though. Or her family and people. It didn't work like that.

"You don't want that male." His voice was a rough rasp.

"It doesn't matter. I have responsibilities. I need to go back and do damage control but first, I'm going to take you up on at least part of your offer." She was in huge shit already, may as well make it worth it. She was going to have to mate Cody in the coming weeks. They would be expected to consummate the mating. She would have to bear young. His young. Demi put her arms around Obsidian's neck. It wasn't something she wanted to think about right then though. "Please, I want you again. One last time." A memory that would have to last her a lifetime.

His jaw was tense. His eyes hard. "Before you are forced to be with some male you—"

"I don't want to talk about any of that anymore. This started as two people attracted to one another. As—"

"Actually, it started as you being terrified of me." He smiled.

"Crazy since you're such a big softy." She reached up on her tippy toes and kissed him gently on the lips.

"Do wolves do that? Is it normal?"

"What?" She narrowed her eyes. "Kissing?"

He nodded.

"I guess it's more of a human thing, but we've become humanized in recent years. Our males have started taking humans as mates due to a shortage of females. All of the species seem to have the problem."

He nodded. "We have the same problem."

"You haven't taken a human though?"

Obsidian shook his head. "They are too timid. I think I might prefer wolves."

She giggled.

"About that kiss you were asking about." He looked down at her lips and her heart did this flip flop thing. "Do you like doing it?"

"What, kissing?"

Obsidian nodded.

"Don't you?" she asked.

"You are the first female to ever…"

She gasped. "You've never been kissed."

He shrugged. "I have."

Demi felt disappointment, which was stupid and yet, there it was. She had wanted to be his first. So stupid, since after today, they would never see each other again.

"You kissed me. That was the third time." Those frown lines were back. He got them every time he was overthinking something.

Oh. Ohhhh! So, she *was* his first then. Demi smiled. "That was nothing. How about this?" She slanted her lips over his and then opened her mouth a little, licked her tongue against the seam of his lips.

Nothing.

She cracked her eyes open a little, only to find that his eyes were still open. He was still frowning. "Don't you like it?"

"I do, but I'm not sure…" He shrugged his big shoulders. She could tell that he didn't know what to do.

"Our lips touch and then we tangle our tongues together." She giggled at how silly it sounded. "You'll like it. I think. You want to try again?"

Instead of answering, he hooked an arm around her waist and pulled her in, sliding his mouth over hers. This time when she pushed her tongue against his lips, his mouth opened. Then they were all lips and tongues. It didn't take Obsidian long to get the hang of it. For him to change angles. For his other hand to thread into the hair on the back of her head. He groaned as he released her.

"How was it?" she asked.

"It makes me want to fuck you."

She laughed. He certainly didn't mince his words. "It's designed to get a person hot and bothered."

"I'm hot, hard and bothered."

She laughed some more. "Let's take care of that then." She gripped his cock in her hand and Obsidian hissed.

He squeezed his eyes closed for a moment. When they opened, they had a look that could easily be mistaken for rage. Obsidian was frowning heavily. Thankfully, it was lust and not anger. She'd hate to be on the receiving end of the other emotion. That was for sure.

His cock twitched in her hand when she gave it a tug.

This time, Obsidian clenched his teeth and growled. Hell's teeth but he was sexy. He kissed her for a second or two… hot and heavy, and then buried his face in her neck, raking his teeth across her skin. A punch of need hit her in the pit of her stomach.

Obsidian picked her up and took a few steps towards the forest before putting her down on her ass on a softer patch of ground. He kneeled in front of her, leaning in and capturing one of her nipples in his hot mouth. Her head fell back as he swirled his tongue around her tight nub.

Demi groaned.

He kissed her belly and then… she all out groaned when he placed a kiss on her clit. Obsidian gripped her thighs firmly in his big hands and lifted them as he closed his mouth over her clit. Her mouth fell open. Using firm strokes of his tongue, he laved her until she was panting.

Demi thread her fingers into his hair. She moaned as his tongue breached her pussy. Moaned even harder when his mouth moved back to her clit where he suckled her. His head bobbed up and down. The sensation was amazing. He let one of her thighs go, Demi hooked her leg over his shoulder, crying out when he thrust his finger into her. Even his hands were big, which meant his fingers… she yelled a second time, louder since he had crooked his finger inside her. Her eyes widened as he picked up the pace. He was rubbing on that spot inside her. His mouth… *Holy hell!* Her orgasm hit her like a punch. Fast and hard. Demi growled low before making a sharp keening noise. Obsidian kept fingering her. His mouth kept working her until she was spent.

"Want you," he groaned. His voice laced with need. It made her ache for more, even though she'd just had an orgasm that rivaled any she'd had to date.

Demi was still struggling to catch her breath when he flipped her onto her knees, his hand moving to her belly.

She remembered him saying he had never taken a female on her back before. What was the chance that any other position, other than this one, would be new to him? "Wait." She looked back at him over her shoulder, catching his frown.

Demi wanted to give him something to remember. For some odd reason it was important to her that he never forget her, or their one night together.

CHAPTER 6

Obsidian had his hands on her hips. He'd been ready to take her. His eyes were on her glistening pussy.

"Wait," the wolf said, a hint of urgency in her voice.

His eyes moved to hers as she looked back at him over her shoulder. He didn't trust himself to speak just then. His voice would barely be human.

"I'd like to try something." She turned around, facing him on her haunches. Demi laughed, he loved the way she looked when she did that. Carefree. Like she didn't have a worry in the world. He wished that was true. Wished even harder that she would let him help her. "Don't look so nervous. Sit on your ass."

Obsidian glanced down at himself. He was on his knees. His cock jutting from his body. His head glistened with seed. His sac had pulled tight with need. "My ass?" A deep, hard growl that would have had any human running.

Not this wolf. She grinned at him. So fucking sexy that he almost came right then. "Sit... yes... on your ass." She quirked up a brow. "Do it." She licked her lips. "Now."

No one had ever told him what to do before. Especially during sex. It was normally a quick coupling, over almost before it began. Obsidian did as she asked. He would do just about anything this female told him to do. As long as she let him inside her body one last time.

One.

Last.

Time.

Why did that thought aggravate him? It made his dragon edgy. His scales rub beneath his skin. Then she was straddling him, her small hands on his chest. Her big, dark eyes on his. She was biting on her plump lower lip. Her hard nipples rubbing up against him as she lifted up.

She gave him this wicked smile and then licked the palm of her hand. A wolf in human skin. Had anything been more attractive to him? Weird! Fucking insane.

No.

This was it, the single most sexy thing he had ever seen. Using the same hand, she fisted his cock. Obsidian grunted loudly as she moved her hand from his tip to his base, sure to spread the seed. More oozed out. Fuck, but too much more of this and he was going to explode before he even got inside her. He tried to clear his mind. Tried to get the scent of her arousal, of her wet pussy, from his snout. Obsidian opened his mouth, breathing through that instead. She tugged on his cock a couple of times, eliciting a deep growl from him. Then she looked him in the eyes as she positioned his tip at her opening.

He snarled as she sank down on him. Her head falling back and her eyes fluttering shut. It took a couple of slow easy thrusts before she was fully seated on him. Those dark eyes were back on him. His cock was squeezed so damned tight it almost hurt.

Almost.

As it stood, the feel of her wrapped around him was the best thing he had ever felt. He gripped her hips, thrusting into her from below, lifting her on and off his cock, nice and easy. He wanted this to last.

She shook her head, her cheeks flushed. "You need to sit still," Demi murmured.

Obsidian grunted in response. Sit still. *What?* He shook his head, wanting more of her, needing—

"I insist," she said between pants. "No moving." She peeled his hands off her hips. "Place them on the ground behind you and lean back a little."

He did as she said. It was difficult. He wanted to touch. Wanted to fuck her more than he wanted to take his next breath. "There. That's better." She ground her pussy onto him, using a little circular motion with her hips that drove him wild with need. Her eyes went all hazy and her mouth dropped open just a little. *Fucking sexy.*

Obsidian grunted loudly, looking down at where they were joined. She lifted just a little, grinding down on him with that circular motion. "Fuck," he managed to push out. In awe at how amazing it felt.

All he wanted to do though was to thrust. To grip her hips. To put her on her back and grind into her. Even better, to put her on her knees so that he could pound into her. The fact that he could do none of these things, the fact that he was at her complete mercy, made this feel even better. It excited him no end.

Then she lifted up, coming straight down. Obsidian snarled. "Glad you're enjoying it," Demi said, her voice husky and deep.

He put a hand on her hip, and she chided him. "Hands on the ground."

Obsidian made a noise of frustration but did as she asked. He could feel the earth beneath his fingers. He watched as she picked up the pace, punching down on his cock now. His eyes moved back to where they were joined. Her pussy was stretched wide, slipping up and down, all over his cock which was covered in her juices. She was making little noises, her face pinched. Her tits shook and jiggled with every movement.

Fucking gorgeous!

So incredible!

By now, Obsidian was grunting hard, barely holding on. He didn't want to finish before her. *Fuck!* Obsidian grit his teeth, closing his eyes. She was too gorgeous. The only problem was that now he could feel more. So much more. The slip and slide of her pussy, tight and wet. The scent of her. Musky wolf and sweet female. He could hear the sucking noise her greedy channel was making as she fisted him.

Those little noises she was making had become louder. More urgent. Not urgent enough.

"Fuck it!" he snarled as he used his thumb on her clit. Her mouth fell open as she gasped. Her eyes actually rolled back when he thrust into her from below, his other hand gripping her hip. Her pussy tightened around him like a vice as she yelled, the sound turning deep and throaty as her pussy spasmed around him. Obsidian roared as his seed ejected from him. His balls so tight, they pulled all the way up into his body. He kept his thumb on her clit, holding her there. Forcing her to come harder… longer. He insisted with his dick as well, pummeling into her.

Demi eventually slumped against him, out of breath. Obsidian kept moving, much slower. *Easy does it…* knowing it was time to pull out, to take her home but struggling to actually do it. "We belong together," he finally said, rubbing a hand down her back.

He felt her shake and then a laugh broke from her. It was lazy sounding. "You mean, we make good fuck-buddies?"

He frowned.

"It's a human term for people who have great sex together but not much of a relationship otherwise. Look," she sighed. "It would have been nice to do this a few more times but I need to get back." She lifted off him, her face serious. Her eyes grave. "I enjoyed our time together. I will definitely think back on this night with fondness."

Fondness.

He wanted to snarl at her use of the word. *Fond.* What kind of a word was that?

"My family will be worried. I've been selfish enough as it is."

"You haven't been selfish," Obsidian tried.

She widened her eyes. "Really? There are males out there right now – my father included – looking for me." She shook her head, swiping a hand across her face. "They will know I rutted another male. They will be angry. I should never have stayed this long. I would appreciate it if you could take me back to where we ran into each other."

He shook his head, watching her brow furrow. "No." His voice was still a thick rasp. It came out sounding angry. Which was fitting since there was some anger inside him because of this whole situation. "I will take you home."

"What?" Her eyes widened. "No, that's fine, you—"

"I insist." Obsidian kept his eyes on her. "It is late. It's…"

"Not you too. You do realize that I'm a grown female? I am so sick of being treated like an idiot because of it."

"I had noticed that you were a female." Obsidian allowed his eyes to drift down to her plump breasts before returning back to her eyes. "I definitely do not see you as an idiot."

"You know what I mean," she snorted.

"I know you are capable of looking after yourself. I had several wounds to prove it." He touched his chest and his side… both areas had long-since healed.

Her cheeks turned a little pink and her mouth turned up at the edges. "Sorry about that."

He shrugged. "I deserved it."

"Don't sneak up on me looking all angry again." She smiled.

"I wasn't angry." He smiled back at her. It felt weird, he couldn't remember the last time he had smiled so much. Obsidian liked talking to this female. He liked the feeling of happiness he felt with her.

"I know that now. Listen," she touched the side of his arm, "you really don't have to take me all the way to my house. Someone might be waiting there for me. In fact, there is a good chance that will be the case."

He took her hand in his and shrugged. "I'm not leaving you out in the forest. You said yourself that you don't stay out at night. I will drop you off and then leave. Not because I don't think you can take care of yourself but because it would be the right thing to do." Obsidian wasn't afraid of a wolf or two. Hell, he'd deal with the entire pack if need be.

"I don't want for there to be trouble. You can drop me somewhere close to home and I'll—"

"I am a big male. I can deal with whatever comes my way." He squeezed her hand. "Your safety is what's most important to me. Your people already know you were with a dragon shifter. They will have been able to scent it."

"Knowing something and seeing it are two different things, but if you're sure…"

"I am. It wouldn't be right otherwise."

"You're a big softy, you know that, right?" she chuckled, putting her arms around his middle.

Anyone who knew him would refute that flat out. Obsidian put his arms around her and tasted her lips. A few minutes later, she groaned and pulled away. "Any more of that and I'll never get home."

"That's the idea." *Why didn't she just stay?* He was sure they could be happy together.

She widened her eyes. "You know I can't. We'd better get going."

He nodded, stepping back so that he could shift. "I know where your village is."

She looked shocked. "There are several shifter villages, do you—"

"I've seen you before."

"Oh really? So you were stalking me?" She raised her brows, folding her arms. He could see she was toying with him but still felt appalled at the idea that she would think that of him.

"Not at all! I have seen you, that's all. A couple of times. The first time I saw you leaving your village a couple of weeks ago. Since then I've come by, kind of hoping to catch a sighting of you. It wasn't in a weird way, though. I guess I like watching you run in your wolf form."

"Oh." Her cheeks turned rosy. "Okay. You knew I was a shifter though."

He nodded. "Yeah, I could tell. You run really fast and,"

he shrugged, "I could see how much you enjoyed being in your wolf form. How in touch you are with your beast. It reminded me of me." He hoped he wasn't sounding like an idiot or a weirdo or something.

She smiled. "You have never seen me in my human form? Not before today at any rate?"

He shook his head.

That seemed to appease her, for whatever reason.

He took one more step back, feeling his dragon break free. Scales sprouted up on his body. His wings lengthened until they were at capacity. He flapped them once, twice, loving the feeling.

Then he took to the sky, reaching down to clasp her around the waist. It didn't take them long to reach her village. Obsidian was sure to stay high until they were right over it. He didn't want to alert her pack to their presence if he could help it. He knew the side of her village that she had exited from and headed for that section, careful to stay silent. "That's my house there." She pointed. "The one with the lights on."

There were very few dwellings with lights on at this late hour. He suspected she was right. Someone was indeed waiting for her.

"We'll need to make our goodbye quick," she whispered as they descended. "I really don't want trouble."

He made a rumbling noise he hoped would soothe her fears. Obsidian landed carefully and shifted back as quickly as he could. He hadn't shifted this often or spent this much time in his human skin in a long time. He found the change easier than he had in a long while.

The female widened her eyes and put a finger over her mouth to hush him. She gestured towards the house.

Obsidian had heard someone moving around inside, even as they descended. He nodded once, taking her hand.

This was it.

The end.

It felt like he had known Demi so much longer. The dragon females had only ever used him for sex on occasion. As he spent more and more time in his scales, they'd visited him less and less. It had been… a long time since he'd rutted one. They never spent any time with him. Never talked to him or cared at all. Not like Demi. She treated him like he was normal.

He'd been on one or two Stag Runs a few years ago, but humans were terrified of him, so that hadn't worked out. This felt… it felt right, and yet everything was against the two of them.

Demi was looking up at him like maybe she was going to miss him as well. Like maybe she had hoped this would go somewhere too. That meant something to him.

"Go," she mouthed, her eyes moving to the sky.

He could still hear whomever it was, moving about in Demi's house. A drawer opened and then closed. Then another was opened.

He gave a quick shake of his head and cupped her jaw in his hand, leaning in to kiss her one last time. She gripped his biceps. His eyes were focused on her mouth. Succulent and sweet tasting. Her eyes were on his mouth as well, they—

"What the fuck is this?" a male snarled from the doorway to her house.

Demi got a frightened look that pissed him the hell off. "It's not what you think," she stammered. Her eyes darted to where the male was standing. She let Obsidian go, acting like her hands were burning and he was the source of the flame.

"You're right it's not what I think," the male said, exiting the house. He had a different scent to Demi. "We thought you had been raped and abducted. What the fuck is going on here? I can't believe this. You actually let this," he sniffed the air, "this beast—"

"Stop!" Obsidian held up a hand. Not liking how this male was talking to Demi. She had said she didn't want trouble. Punching this loser in the face would be just that. Trouble.

"You can fuck right off." The male pointed at Obsidian. "While you still have a chance that is."

"You should go," Demi said, sounding panicked.

"Are you going to be okay?" He felt his whole demeanor soften as he looked back down at her.

"Of course she will be okay, you dragon asshole!" the male snarled. "Demi is back where she belongs, with her own kind."

"Stop it, Cody!" she interrupted, sounding angry.

Oh, fucking great! This was that Cody male. Obsidian turned back to him, looking at him with new eyes. The male was big for a shifter, maybe because he was a bear rather than a wolf. His shoulders were wide, his arms thick. He wore a pair of jeans and nothing else. His hair was a light color. His eyes as well. The dragon females would find him very attractive. He had the sort of looks females of all species enjoyed. Pity he was such a prick.

"You should really go now," Demi urged.

"Yes, listen to the female... *my* female," Cody pointed at his chest, "my fucking female and you can fuck off." That finger pointed back at Obsidian, who wanted to break it. This male was aggravating him in a big way. All he had wanted was to see Demi home safely and to say goodbye to her.

"I'm not yours, Cody, I haven't agreed to anything," Demi threw back. "Stop saying that I'm your female."

Obsidian couldn't help the grin that took up residence on his face.

"I'm not yours either," she said, looking back at him.

He forced the smile off his face. Again, not wanting to cause trouble.

"You *are* mine!" the prick yelled, that finger pointing back at Demi. He wanted to break it so badly.

She shook her head. "Not even close. It's ultimately my decision and I haven't made one either way. In fact, you know my feelings on this. They do not align with yours."

"How can you say that? The lives of our—"

Demi put up a hand. "I know, okay? I know. I don't need to keep hearing the same thing over and over. 'The lives of our people are at stake. Keeping the peace is important. What about tradition?' I've heard it all before."

"You obviously do need to hear it again, Demi, because it's not sinking in. I can't believe this." The male ran a hand through his hair. His eyes blazed. "I can't believe I ever said that you reminded me of her. That I ever thought it." He widened his eyes, his nostrils flaring with obvious anger.

Obsidian hoped that this conversation wasn't going in the direction that he thought it was. Because all bets were off then. Trouble would be out in full fucking force.

Demi must have seen him bristle. He'd definitely clenched his jaw and closed his fists. He'd taken a step towards the male and might even have growled.

"Go, Obsidian!" Demi pleaded but he was obviously a sick fuck because he needed to hear the rest of what this asshole had to say.

"You are nothing like my precious Brie." Maybe if the male had looked upset, Obsidian could have forgiven the outburst. Instead, his eyes narrowed in hate. "My Brie would never have fucked around with a filthy dragon."

"Don't say any more, Cody. Don't!" Demi warned.

"We're about to be mated. How could you? Do you expect me to take you to my bed now? After this?"

Obsidian's chest heaved. He heard his molars crack he ground them so hard, but he kept himself in check. "You don't want to stay with this prick," he finally managed to say to her, his voice thick and corded. "You need to stop disrespecting Demi," he directed at the bear shifter There was a rough edge to his voice. This bear had better take the warning and stop.

"What did you call me?" Cody took two strides towards him. That finger pointing.

"Don't!" Demi spoke to the other male but put a hand on Obsidian's chest as she said it.

The prick exhaled, his shoulders relaxing. "Why am I even bothering? You *will* mate me," he said to Demi before turning back to Obsidian. "I'm the one who will get to fuck her every night. Me, dragon! Not you!" His eyes gleamed with malice. He turned to Demi, that fucking finger still pointing. At her now though. "It's a bunch of bullshit about you having a say in the matter, Demi. You don't! It's happening… tomorrow. Whether you like it or not. The sooner I get this fucker's scent off you and your belly full of my cubs the better."

There was only so much a male could take. Obsidian saw red.

CHAPTER 7

Obsidian snarled. The sound terrifying. Even Cody –
Alpha of the Vale Creek packs – paled. His mouth
opened like a fish out of water as Obsidian charged
at him. Demi didn't have time to try to stop him. To say or
to do anything. Neither did Cody, who was about to take the
brunt of all that anger. He tried to sidestep the huge dragon
male but was far too slow. Obsidian shoulder-tackled him.
There was a loud thudding noise as one hard body hit
another. Obsidian must be the harder of the two, because
Cody went flying. Literally. His body came off the ground as
he flew back for a few feet before crashing down hard. All
the air left him, as he made a *humph* sound.

Then he just lay there for a few long seconds. His eyes
were wide. His mouth open. Cody rolled to the left and then
back to the right.

"He's winded," Obsidian said. "I also might have cracked
a rib… or two. The dickhead deserved it."

His head cocked to the side and he glanced to the right of
her. "There are more males approaching." Obsidian looked

back at her. His eyes holding hers for a second. "You should think very carefully before mating a male like that. I know I have no say in the matter, but you will never be happy."

She shook her head. "Don't judge him. I know it looks bad. He's just angry and not thinking straight. He's still cut up over Brie."

Obsidian frowned, wanting to say something, but Cody sucked in a deep, gasping breath.

Now she could hear the footfalls as well. They didn't have more than a couple of seconds. "He isn't a bad male, he's just… sad." She shrugged. "He's ultimately right though, about everything."

"Right, my ass!" he all but snarled. "There's nothing wrong with you."

"Not about that," she spoke quickly. Time was running out. "About my fate being sealed. Despite what he said, he won't harm me or force me. I promise." She pushed at his chest. "Go now. If they catch you…" She shook her head. "Please, I don't want to see you hurt."

"They couldn't hurt me," he snorted.

"They can. A whole pack of them would kill you. Go! Please." She reached up and kissed him, softly. Ever so softly.

Obsidian nodded, he swallowed thickly. "I will miss you, Demi. Have a good life."

She nodded back, wanting to tell him the same, but he shifted in a second flat and vanished into the sky with just a few hard flaps of his great wings.

Cody staggered to his feet. He was clutching at his chest, which had a purple stain across several ribs. His face was sweaty and contorted with pain.

Several Betas rounded the corner. "What happened? We

heard yelling and snarling," the closest of them said, his eyes narrowed, and he sniffed the air. "Are you hurt?" he directed the question at her, eyes on hers. "Do I need to get a healer?"

"I'm fine." She folded her arms across her chest, feeling vulnerable in her skin. Nudity was normal amongst her kind. The Betas were naked as well, but right then, she just wanted to get inside and away from everything and everyone.

"Leave!" Cody spat.

A second Beta frowned, sniffing the air.

This agitated Cody even more. "Go now. Send word to Demi's father that she is safe. He is with the tracking party to the north of our village," Cody instructed.

"There is more than one tracking party?" She knew they would be worried but to have several tracking parties out there looking for her seemed extreme.

The Beta nodded. "Are you sure you are alright?" he asked her again, looking like he didn't believe her.

"You heard our Alpha," the bear shifter snarled.

"Butt out," the wolf Beta snarled back. "I'm checking in on the female."

"She's fine!" Cody snapped.

The wolf Beta's frown deepened, and his nostrils flared. "Why does she…?"

"Go now! My father is out there as well. Demi is perfectly fine, despite our initial deduction."

"Oh," the wolf male said. "Ohhhh!" he drew out the word, his eyes widening.

"Oh shit!" the bear Beta snickered, realizing what she'd been up to. Demi felt her cheeks heat but kept her shoulders back and her chin tilted up. She had done nothing wrong.

"Fuck off before I…" Cody drew himself to his full

height. His cracked ribs forgotten.

The male who had laughed looked down at his feet. All of them left hurriedly. If they could have had their tails between their legs, they would have. Demi could hear them bickering amongst themselves as they ran off.

"Let's go inside." Cody was frowning.

She nodded.

As soon as they were inside, she turned to face him. "What's going on?" Demi frowned. Not sure she wanted to know the answer to her own question. "Why are there several search parties out looking for me?"

"We scented blood and rutting, what do you think we imagined had happened in that clearing."

Shit! His earlier words came back to her. Demi hadn't thought they would assume the worst. "Why did you even come after me in the first place? Wait a minute, why are you here?"

"I was with the original search party. There when we walked in on the clearing. We heard him run off with you. We heard you scream. You said 'No'! We all heard you, Demi. We've been out of our minds with worry, and all this time you were…" He ground his teeth.

"I'm sorry," she whispered. "I—"

"Sorry doesn't cut it. Your father is out there now. Your mother is crying and inconsolable. She thinks he raped you."

"Okay. Shit! Okay." She shook her head. "I said I was sorry. I'm a mature female, way past the age of mating. I'm a wolf shifter, more than capable of taking care of myself."

"Not against that." Cody pointed straight up into the sky.

"I guess…" She sighed. "I guess I didn't think it through." She was a terrible person to have put them through this. "It had all become too much for me. The pressure was—"

"Am I so bad?" Cody got this look, like a lost little boy.

"No! That's not it."

"You wouldn't say so by the way you act. I could have my pick of females. They run after me, waving their asses in the air on a daily basis. I haven't so much as laid a paw on any of them. Not one. Not in all this time."

"I haven't let anyone touch me either," she countered.

"Until today," he growled. "I'm going to be the laughing stock of both packs."

"I said I was sorry. I don't want this Cody. We don't belong together. You can't deny that. I felt trapped. I *feel* trapped. When I was out there, with the dragon, I felt free for the first time in a long time. I haven't felt anything like it for the longest time." She shrugged. "Except for pain and sorrow. Nothing else but those emotions, and then today, I did. I felt… something more…" Her eyes prickled with unshed tears. "I…"

"I don't want to hear another word about the dragon," his voice boomed. "We are mating. It's happening, Demi."

"We can change their minds. Some traditions can evolve. You can make that decision now, as the new Alpha."

"No! We are mating. I choose you." He grabbed her hands, quickly dropping them again. His nostrils flaring.

"I don't want this."

"It's happening. I meant what I said to the dragon. We are expected to mate and to have cubs."

"I know," she mumbled. "I know." Clearer that time. "But you need to know that I don't love you in that way." She winced, feeling bad for Cody. "I *never* will."

"You are fucking this up before we even begin," he snarled. "Why can't you just give it a try? One fucking try,

Demi."

"You don't belong to me. You're Brie's!" she shouted. Why did no one understand that? How was it that Cody didn't get that? He used to.

"Brie is dead. She's gone." His eyes blazed. She wasn't sure whether it was with tears or anger. Maybe a mix of both.

"Don't!" she begged. "Please."

"I'm sorry to be so blunt, but it's the truth. We're here. We're alive. We deserve happiness."

"You're right. We do, but not together. Why can't you see that anymore?" Demi had preferred it when they worked as a team against this farce of a mating. Why was Cody suddenly insisting on this?

"It's how it has to be," he growled. The words full of emotion. "There is no other option. I have come to accept that, and you must too."

"Fine." Her shoulders slumped as the fight left her. They had stood a chance at getting out of this when they were united. There was no way she would get out of this alone. "I will mate you. If I am forced, I will concede. I'll go through with it."

"You make it sound like a death sentence." Definitely pain in his words.

"It's not that. I told Obsidian you weren't a bad person. I meant it. The truth is that I see you as more of a brother."

"It could change," he tried, raising his brows.

"It will *never* change. You need to know that upfront. Open and honest. Like you pointed out, there are many females who feel very differently about you. Why don't you pick one of them? Pick a wolf female and—"

"No! You are the next Alpha female of the wolf pack. It has to be you. My offspring will be strong. The only way to assure that is to mate with the strongest wolf female. We will mate tomorrow. If you refute me in any way, I will make trouble for your dragon. The beast came onto our territory uninvited. He touched what wasn't his to touch. There was blood in that clearing, Demi. Your blood."

"Don't you dare! It wasn't like that."

"You aren't thinking clearly after your ordeal with the creature." His jaw tightened. "Maybe the beast threatened you to keep quiet about what really went down. We might need to let the facts speak for themselves. Blood... seed... an aggressive dragon." He pointed at the blossoming bruising on his ribs.

"No!" she yelled. "You're twisting this."

"The creature came onto our territory and helped itself to one of our females. To *my* female. Even if he didn't force you, it's still an offense. I will make sure the scaly fuck pays. Don't try me. We mate tomorrow." Cody turned and walked out.

Demi's chest heaved. Adrenaline coursed through her veins. She couldn't stop it from happening. Couldn't stop the fur that pushed through her skin. Or her muscles from lengthening and roping. Once the shift was complete, Demi tossed her head back, a long, drawn-out howl filled her house. She howled again and again, until her throat was hoarse. Until she fell asleep, exhausted. Waking only hours later from the nightmare that plagued her every night. Her sister's death. That laughing. His terrible laughing as she died.

CHAPTER 8

Obsidian landed. He was so agitated it took him at least half a minute to shift back into his skin. What he needed was a hot shower, a belly full of food, and sleep. Maybe he would feel better once the sun came up.

Doubtful.

He felt bad for Demi. What kind of a life would she have to look forward to with a jerk like that male? Not much of a one. By the sounds of things, he was going to turn her into a baby-making vessel. Pretty much enslave her.

He held back a roar. No wonder she scented so strongly of fear when he had met her. Everything in him screamed to shift, to go back and to rescue her. Whether she wanted rescuing or not. He hated how she had defended and protected the bear. *Hated!* Maybe if he whisked her away for a couple of days, she would be able to think more clearly. To think she had defended that Cody asshole. Saying that the male was good.

He gave his head a hard shake. Obsidian was too tired to think straight right then. Food and an hour or two of sleep, and he'd be ready to take the next step. Whatever that ended up being.

He dialed the kitchen and put an order in. Then he paced his chamber for a couple of minutes, trying to calm the fuck down before heading to the bathroom. He turned the faucets on, waiting until steam filled the shower stall. Then he got in and began to wash off.

The shower door banged open, almost torn off its hinges in the process.

"What the hell did you do?" his brother snarled.

"Nothing!" he growled back, soap from his hair leaking into his eyes. He tried to put his head under the water, but Mountain yanked him by his arm, pulling him from the stall. Obsidian growled low, allowing himself to be led. His brother was naked… he had recently shifted.

"Nothing, my fucking ass. I can scent a wolf female on you. All over you. You've been rutting. Oh my fuck!" He got a terrified look, his eyes widening. "It's true! It's fucking true!" Mountain turned and walked away from him, both his hands in his hair. "I thought there had to be a mix-up but there isn't one."

"Yes. I rutted. So?" Obsidian grunted.

"You forced yourself on a female, Obsidian. That's not okay."

"I didn't!" Obsidian boomed. "I would never!" he added.

"The wolves scented blood from both of you. That, and rutting. Your seed was on the ground. They could scent fear."

"They would have scented pleasure as well," Obsidian countered. "I gave Demi pleasure."

"Fuck!" Mountain snarled. "That's your excuse? Really? You made her come, so it wasn't rape?"

That word again. That prick Cody had used it too. Then it dawned on him. They really thought he had raped and abducted Demi. He shook his head, feeling anger well. Anger and disappointment. That all the shifters would think badly of him was one thing. That his own people would think it, he could still stomach, but his own twin? Not a chance. "Do you not know me, brother?"

"What the hell does that that even mean?"

"It's a simple question."

"I *do* know you," Mountain spoke using a tender voice. "I'm sure you didn't think you were doing anything wrong. Maybe your beast took over in that moment… maybe…"

"You can stop there." Obsidian put up a hand. "I would never force a female. My beast knows right from wrong. I would never!"

"Not knowingly. You've spent too much time in your scales. It affects a male. It… Wait a minute…" He narrowed his eyes. "You haven't grunted once. You're talking."

Obsidian shrugged. "I'm trying to tell you that… yes, I ran into the female. She was afraid of me and fought me. She injured herself trying to run away. I never laid a claw on her though. Would never hurt an innocent. I'm not so far gone! Not nearly as much as you think. It didn't take long for her to realize I meant no harm. For her to become as aroused as well…"

"You can spare me the details."

"We did rut, but it was consensual. I swear to you! She was fearful of me initially but that soon changed. The fear those shifter males could scent was because of them. It had nothing to do with me by then. We had resolved our differences… twice," he added, unnecessarily.

"The last word we got from them was that they heard you

leave with her. Heard her scream 'No.'"

Obsidian frowned. "She wanted me to leave her to her fate and to just go, but I couldn't. I needed to know what was going on. Why she was so afraid and upset."

"Are you sure it had nothing to do with you?" Mountain asked.

Obsidian bristled. "Very fucking sure! She slept in my arms. That's not the action of someone who has just been raped. Not a fuck!"

His brother raised his brows. "Did you know that she is promised to the new bear Alpha? That they are to be mated?"

"She doesn't want the male though. She is being forced to mate him. He is a prick!"

"Listen to yourself. We can't involve ourselves with the politics of another species. You are in such deep shit, Obsidian. You will need to go and explain yourself to our king. Probably to Blaze as well. You might be caged for this, or worse."

"Why?" he growled. "I did nothing wrong. Demi is a mature female, quite capable of making her own decisions."

"She wasn't yours to take."

Obsidian shrugged. "I couldn't scent another male on her. No claim had been made. Demi will set the record straight. That asshole, Cody, saw us in an intimate moment as we were saying goodbye. He will have seen that—"

"Holy fucking shit!" Mountain put a hand through his hair, which was mussed. "An intimate moment you were having with *his* female. The shifters might just call for your blood after this, even if you didn't force her or harm her."

"Fuck that!" Obsidian snarled. "I did nothing wrong. I rutted a female who has never been claimed. I didn't know about the asshole male... Cody," he spat the name. "I took her so that I could get to the bottom of her fear and sadness, only to find out that she is being forced to mate that asshole. I am going to eat and sleep, then I am going to rescue her."

"If you do that," Mountain looked grave, "not even I will be able to protect you. As it stands, I can plead your case. Who knows what bullshit those shifters will come back with. There's a good chance they're angry enough to cause shit for you. Big shit!"

"Let them."

"This is serious. Forcing a female is an offense grave enough to have you beheaded. Granite might be forced to sentence you to death. Or to stand by while they carry out your sentence."

"Demi would never—"

"Your wolf would have no say in the matter," his brother sounded worried.

Was Mountain right? "I did nothing wrong," he repeated. The words sounding hollow.

"I know." His brother squeezed his shoulder. "I'm sorry I doubted you. This all needs to be explained to our king. Before we even head there though, you need to stop talking about going back to this female. It will never be permitted. That wolf—"

"Her name is Demi." He held back a snarl of frustration.

"Demi." His brother's voice softened. "I can see that you have come to care for her in a short time. You need to forget about her though. You can't allow yourself to get in too deep with her."

"What will happen to her?"

"I'm sure she's going to be in serious trouble as well."

Obsidian growled, low and deep. Wanting to snarl. To

roar and to rail. Wanting to shift and to go to her.

"Stop that! Get a grip." Mountain's eyes narrowed. "She isn't yours. She never will be."

"They are going to force her to—"

"It is out of our claws. There is nothing we can do. Do you hear me? If you go anywhere near her, you are sealing your fate. As it stands, you might be in deep trouble but if you go there, if you touch her, you *will* be." He shrugged, looking frustrated. "We won't be able to protect you. *I* won't be able to protect you. You didn't know who she was promised to earlier. That she is the bear Alpha's promised mate. You do now."

"But—"

"But nothing! Finish your shower. Get dressed and let's go and see Granite. I need to get back to my mate." Mountain got a goofy look on his face. It quickly turned stern. "We haven't even consummated our mating. Page isn't officially mine, yet I was out searching for you when I got word you were back. I've been out there for hours, worried sick that you'd made a mistake and hurt that female."

"I would never—"

"I know, I should never have doubted you."

"I'm sorry," Obsidian pushed the words out. "I screwed up your night."

"I'm glad this didn't go down in the way they are saying. We'll sort it out." Mountain patted his back.

Sort it out. Sorting it out would mean helping Demi. It didn't feel like anything had been sorted out. A heaviness settled inside of him. Obsidian forced himself to nod once in agreement.

CHAPTER 9

Demi was thankful for the lacy veil that covered her head. So thankful it covered her eyes, which were puffy and red. It didn't matter how much she had cried already. Fresh tears still welled. How was it even possible?

Her lip quivered as well. She'd never been a weakling. Never given in to so much self-pity before. It was nauseating and yet… there it was. No escape! Not even from herself.

"All will be well," her father spoke in a soothing voice. "I'm almost glad this whole debacle happened. It moved things along. Let's go." He sighed deeply. "Despite what you may think, I do love you. I know that Cody will take good care of you." His eyes were focused on where Cody was waiting for them at the end of the aisle. An aisle formed by all the people of their packs. The bear shifter stood beneath an arch of flowering roses, looking dapper in his tuxedo. The male had gone to a lot of effort and yet… nothing. Only more sorrow. Sorrow that Brie wasn't there. Her sister should be there, dammit! Sorrow that she was, and at the unfairness of the whole situation. She even felt sorry for Cody. He didn't deserve this either. At the same time, she was angry with him for his manipulation. He was using what happened to get his way. It was wrong.

"You will grow to love him back." Her father squeezed her arm and began to walk.

Grow to love him. Panic welled as she was forced to follow. Her legs heavy.

She had loved Cody once as a brother. Demi struggled to summon an ounce of that love right then. Even if it did come back one day, it would still be brotherly love. She could never love him as a male. Certainly not as a lover. Not anything along those lines. Being with the dragon shifter had only highlighted that fact for her.

By all the gods, but her skin itched with the need to shift. Her limbs wanted to stretch out with the change and then even more as she ran and ran and ran. Far away from there. From this.

She swallowed hard as they entered the aisle. Everyone from their village gathered. All of their eyes on her. Cody was frowning. His normally bright eyes were dark and brooding. The tuxedo pulled tight around his chest and arms. He forced a tight smile that didn't even come close to reaching his eyes as she and her father drew nearer.

Her dad kissed her cheek through the veil. He patted her arm. She could hear her mother crying quietly behind them. She had tried to convince her mom to help her. To stop this, but she was not to be swayed either.

Cody took her hand in his and they both faced the elder before them, who greeted first them and then the crowd. He said a few words in opening that were a complete blur to Demi. She had to concentrate to keep herself from openly crying.

A few minutes in, Cody squeezed her hand and she realized that the elder had asked her a question. "Um… yes," she blurted. Her voice a touch shrill.

A couple of people in the crowd gasped. Several more whispered amongst themselves.

"You're supposed to say no," Cody whispered, giving her hand another squeeze.

"I asked if there was a reason why the two of you should not mate?" The elder smiled. He was very sweet. His hair was salt and pepper and his eyes were a watery blue. But his smile was kind.

Cody squeezed her hand again.

"Oh!" she exclaimed. "No." She shook her head too hard. Only because there were so many reasons why they shouldn't be doing this.

The elder asked the same of Cody who answered immediately. He lied as well, saying that there was no reason why they shouldn't be mated. She was being forced into this. That should be reason enough. This was a silly human tradition they had adopted. Why, she didn't know, since it didn't matter how they answered. She tried to concentrate on what he was saying.

"I need you both to repeat after me in unison. When you speak, it will be each to one and the other." The priest bowed his head, his eyes shut. "Let us begin," he paused. "To you, I give of myself."

Demi squeezed her eyes shut and said the words. She tried not to think too hard about what she was saying.

"My fur is your fur," he went on.

They both repeated the words. Sounding like robots. Demi felt more and more numb inside. Cody's hand began to feel sweaty. Maybe she was the one doing the sweating.

"My life is your life," the elder said.

Again, they repeated. Cody squeezed her hand as he spoke, she could feel him looking at her. *Hold it together!* she repeated to herself.

"Together as one in this life as well as the next," the elder said.

How could she say those words? *How?*

Cody said them, faltering when she didn't. She heard him swallow hard, heard him lick his lips.

"Together…" she forced, "in this life…" A sob left her. *Shit!* She had to do this. Demi heard her mom cry harder, blowing her nose. Demi cleared her throat. "As well as the next." It made her think of Brie, which made her cry all over again. *Flip!* Tears streamed down her cheeks. Thankfully no one could see through the lace of the veil.

"Shall we do the blood-joining ceremony to consummate the union?" The elder removed and unsheathed a dagger. It was a plain gold blade with a bone handle.

For a moment she was stunned, her eyes glued to the glinting blade. Blood-joining was more of a vampire tradition. One the other species used sometimes. "No!" She shook her head. "No… um… thank you," she quickly added.

The elder raised a brow. "I assure you it won't hurt. It… Your father said that…"

"No," Cody said. "We appreciate the sentiment, but we will consummate the mating in… the usual fashion. Thank you, but no."

"As you wish." The elder bowed his head and put the knife back into the sheath. He went on to tell a story that Demi barely heard.

"And now," the elder clutched his hands together, "we have come to my favorite part. With the rising of the sun, Cody of the bear pack and Demi of the wolf pack, you will be mated."

Dread filled her. This was not how she envisioned this moment. Her blood running cold. Disbelief rising with the passing of each second. It was stupid but she'd somehow thought that this moment wouldn't come. That someone would stop it. Cody, her father, her mother... someone. *Him.* Had she been expecting the dragon shifter? Had she somehow expected Obsidian to swoop down and save her?

The elder said something she didn't hear. Demi turned to leave but Cody put a hand on her hip, turning her to him. "We must kiss," he said.

Oh!

Right!

She took a steadying breath, looking up at him through the lace. He was such a handsome male. Ultimately a good male. She wished hard, and not for the first time, that she felt something for him. Just thinking that brought fresh waves of guilt.

Cody lifted her veil, allowing it to fall down her back. He frowned, his jaw tightening. Fresh tears tracked down her cheeks. He leaned in, placing a kiss on the corner of her mouth. The whole thing was over in half a second and lord help her, but it had her heaving out a sigh of relief. He took her hand and they turned towards the crowd.

This was normally when the whole village would erupt with cheers, shouts and catcalls. Not today. They rose to their feet and clapped. The air was serious, too serious.

Demi worked hard to hold it together as they walked down the aisle. Her mother gave her a tight hug. "I'm so sorry," she whispered, sniffing.

"It's okay," she said past the lump in her throat. It wasn't her mother's fault.

Her father hugged her as well, whispering something to her that she didn't register.

Next, she hugged Serge. His expression reminded her of the day they had buried Brie. Just as grave.

Lastly, she embraced her new family. First her mother-in-law and then her new father. She responded with a nod when they offered words of welcome. Every eye glued on them. She didn't look left or right, or at any individual face. Everything was a blur. She felt completely numb.

Should she tell Cody she wasn't feeling well? That she needed to lie down? She couldn't handle trying to make small-talk with everyone at the gathering. They were supposed to be happy and celebrating. Instead, her stomach churned at the thought of food. Her heart felt heavy.

On the other hand, she needed to delay being alone with Cody for as long as possible. She didn't think that she could handle what… would be expected of her.

Cody turned to her slightly as they walked. "Let's head home," he whispered.

She nodded once, not trusting her voice. The walk to their new residence took forever and at the same time it felt like mere moments. Demi wanted to hide away but didn't want to be alone with Cody. The thought terrified her.

The cottage they had been gifted was beautiful. It was a quaint three-bedroom stone and thatch double-story that bordered the forest and had a quaint garden and orchard.

"Brie would have loved this." The words came out before she could stop them.

"Yeah, she would have." His voice was wistful. "We will

too," he added, injecting something else. Something forceful.

Demi didn't say anything.

Cody opened the door for her and stood to the side. As soon as the door was closed, he took off his jacket, hanging it over the back of a chair. Then he unbuttoned his cuffs. "We'd better get this over and done with."

The air seized in her lungs as she watched him take his shirt off. "Get what over and done with?"

"You know exactly what I'm talking about." He unbuttoned the top button of his pants. "We need to consummate this mating." His eyes blazed and his jaw was tight.

CHAPTER 10

S tone's eyes brightened as they landed on him. "Glad you could make it." He smiled for half a second before he turned back into the serious team leader he was.

Obsidian nodded. He grunted once. He was there, not for any other reason than that his brother had asked it of him. He owed Mountain for dragging him out of his mating bed the night before. So, when Obsidian had received the call to ask him to attend training this afternoon, he'd been obligated to be there. A waste of time, if you asked him. He was strong and fast. Better than every male in attendance. Training was obsolete. Training was for those who needed it. *Not for him!* His brother would argue that it had to do with teamwork. *Blah blah blah…* All hot air. He was already bored. Already itching to be in his scales and he'd only just arrived.

"We're going to focus on aerial combat," Stone addressed the group of males, most of whom groaned at the news.

Aerial combat. *Good!* Now this was a training session he could get into. He'd be able to take out some of his frustrations. He clicked his knuckles, eliciting a couple of dirty looks from the males closest to him.

"You all know the rules. I don't have to go through them with you. You are no longer whelps." Stone let his eyes drift over the crowd.

"Maybe you should, just to be on the safe side," Clay said, his red hair giving him away immediately. He glanced back at Obsidian as he spoke, a deep frown creasing his brow.

"You all know the rules." Stone sounded a strange mix of both bored and irritated.

"Some of us don't come to training very often," Clay growled out the words. "Maybe we've forgotten. Maybe we need reminding." He clenched his jaw, his eyes still on Obsidian. He'd broken the asshole's leg once. It had been an accident. *Boo fucking hoo!* Clay was such a loser.

"Has anyone forgotten the rules?" Stone allowed his eyes to drift across the crowd once again. "Anyone?" he added unnecessarily as his gaze landed on Obsidian, where it stayed for a few beats. "That's what I thought." He nodded once. "We're not whelps," he muttered again under his breath. "This is a training session… not a war zone. That's pretty much all you have to keep in mind."

"Yeah, right!" Clay grumbled, shaking his head.

"All that is left," Stone ignored the male, "is to decide on sparring pairs. Pick someone quickly."

Obsidian folded his arms across his chest and rolled his eyes. This was the part where everyone did as Stone said, except, no one would pick him. They never did. *Bunch of pussies!* So he had broken a couple of bones when he was younger. Didn't mean it would happen again. The males quickly partnered up. No one approached him. *Big surprise!*

Clay shoulder-bashed his partner a little too hard. It was Ore. A male much smaller in stature. Trust Clay to orchestrate an unfair partnership. One which assured him victory. It was stupid too, since Clay was a big male. He was good too. He didn't need to always take the easy road. Poor Ore went flying into the males next to him, who thankfully kept him from falling.

Stone got an unsettled look, his jaw tightening for a moment. Then he turned back to the general crowd. "Anyone aside from Obsidian and Flint who doesn't have a partner?"

Obsidian had to bite back a laugh when he saw the look on Flint's face. The male was shitting himself. This was why he didn't come to training very often. He'd go easy on the male. He'd remember the rules and obey them.

"Okay." Stone nodded once. "I want to change things up though. Clay…" he pointed to the male, "I want you to team up with Obsidian."

Clay narrowed his eyes. "Ore and I have already—"

"This isn't a discussion," Stone growled. "Clay, I want you with Obsidian. Flint and Ore, the two of you are against one another."

Great! At least Clay would be better competition. The male in question muttered a curse under his breath.

"Obsidian knows the rules. He will obey them," Stone said.

"Like hell!" Clay grumbled under his breath. "Fucking savage," he muttered some more.

"It will…" Stone began. "Oh." He frowned. "I didn't expect to see you today." His eyes had moved to the rear of the balcony, where they focused on someone. "Welcome."

Obsidian followed his line of vision, turning to face the back. Mountain stood in the door opening, his expression grave. Their eyes locked for a moment before Mountain turned his attention back to Stone. "I need a quick word with Obsidian."

Stone nodded. "Of course. We'll get started. Clay, I suggest you start warming up." He smiled.

The male muttered some more curses and shook his head. The sound of the males shifting filled the balcony as Obsidian made his way to his brother.

"It sounds like Clay is excited about your sparring session," Mountain said.

Obsidian put his hands on his hips. "I had planned on going easy on Flint. Clay on the other hand…" He raised his brows.

Mountain laughed. "Please don't do anything stupid."

"I won't! I'll mess with him a little though. He needs to be brought down some. Did you enjoy the rest of your evening?"

"Evening?" Mountain snorted. "It was early morning by the time I made it back to Page." His eyes grew stormy. "She was already asleep, but I enjoyed a glorious morning with my mate."

"So, it's official."

"Yes," Mountain grinned, "it's most definitely official.

Obsidian grunted. "What made you get out of bed then?"

Mountain lost his goofy grin in an instant. "Something… something shitty." He scratched his forehead.

"Tell me."

"It's the wolf female," he said, a strange expression on his face.

"Demi." His heart beat faster. "Did something happen to her? Is everything okay? Did that—"

Mountain held up his hand. "You are immediately

concerned for her wellbeing," Mountain shook his head, "when you should be concerned for yourself."

"Why? I am fine. I—"

"The wolves did not take kindly to what happened. Her father was still calling for your head this morning, even after her safe return."

"Why?" Obsidian growled, his scales rubbing. "I didn't— "

"I know," Mountain used a soothing tone. "We discussed this, and I believe you. It looks like things have been resolved though." Something flashed in Mountain's eyes.

Obsidian wasn't sure what it was. He set his jaw, not liking where this was going. "How has it been resolved?"

"The female mated with the bear shifter earlier today." There it was again. That look. Obsidian realized that it was pity. His brother pitied him.

Anger. Disappointment. Frustration. More anger. "They forced her!" He clenched his fists.

"I am told that it was her choice and that she willingly mated with the male."

"They're lying!" he growled. "They made her do it somehow. I know it." Just like he knew his own damned name.

"It has nothing to do with us," Mountain spoke in soft soothing tones. "I told you this because I didn't believe you when you said you would stay away. You *need* to stay away from her." Mountain clutched his arm. "She is no longer your concern. She has a mate. The wolf, Demi, belongs to the bear shifter now. You dodged a bullet here. I see this as a positive."

Obsidian bit back a snarl.

"I feel bad for you, but at the same time, this takes the

pressure off. You have to stay away!" Mountain's hand clutched him a little tighter. "Please."

Everything in him bristled. Adrenaline surged. He pulled away from Mountain. "I need to get to training."

"Take the day off rather. Tomorrow is another day."

"I can't!" Obsidian growled. "Clay is waiting for me." He pointed at the sky where the male was circling.

"Are you okay? You only spent a handful of hours with this female. It wasn't serious."

Like hell it wasn't!

At least to him. His dragon had recognized something in the female. Something special. Obsidian nodded once, despite feeling that way.

"Now that you're... more *you* again, you should think about going on another Stag Run."

"I was banned. Humans are afraid of me, remember?"

"You seem far less... feral. That female was good for you. Even after such a short time. There are positives in this."

Demi had been amazing for him.

The best.

"I'll talk to Granite. About going again."

Obsidian grunted, not sure how to respond. He didn't want to go on a Stag Run but he didn't want to seem ungrateful either.

"I will see you in a couple of days. I want to spend some quality time with my mate."

Obsidian nodded.

"Stay out of trouble. I'm so glad you're doing better." Mountain grinned, looking relaxed.

Obsidian tried to smile but his teeth wouldn't unclench. They said their goodbyes and he watched as Mountain walked away.

Obsidian looked up at the dragon above. Clay gave a loud roar, clearly telling him to hurry the fuck up. Obsidian contemplated shifting and getting the hell out of there, but Clay roared again. This time smoke wafted from the male's nostrils.

Okay then.

Obsidian shifted in a second flat. The pants he had been wearing shredded from his body as he changed. He had forgotten he was wearing them since he hardly ever donned clothing. It took him a few seconds to reach the male. He sucked in a deep breath, trying hard to temper his emotions.

As much as he wanted to take his frustrations out on this asshole, it would be a mistake. He couldn't believe that she had gone through with it. As much as she insisted that it was the direction she was going in, he just hadn't thought she'd do it. Saying you were going to do something and actually doing it were two very different things.

That bear shifter—Obsidian snarled as Clay bashed into him. The male's claw catching his underbelly. He could scent blood. His own. *Fuck!*

One hard flap of his wings and he was rebalanced. His focus moving to Clay, who was already coming at him again. So much for this being a friendly encounter. He moved aside at the last second and lashed out at Clay, smelling fresh blood again. This time Clay's. *Much better!*

Clay howled in both pain and anger. He roared as he came at Obsidian. Every muscle was bunched. His claws out in full force. Even the male's teeth were bared in a snarl. Again, Obsidian moved, dropping at the last second, just missing those razor-sharp claws by half an inch. Clay growled in frustration. Obsidian growled as well; a warning. His dragon was already agitated. It wanted him to down this fucker and to head for wolf territory. It urged Obsidian to see for himself what was going on with Demi.

Clay came at him again. The male was allowing anger to take over. It had always been his one major weakness. He wasn't thinking rationally anymore. Clay hated Obsidian. He had done so ever since Obsidian had beat him out, finishing top of their class. Obsidian may have accidentally broken the male's leg to get there. Clay had always been an obnoxious prick. His mouth and his temper too big for his own good. Nothing much had changed over the years.

Obsidian moved away. He wanted to give Clay some space. Wanted him to cool down. His own adrenaline was pumping. A good dose of testosterone flooded his system. Clay didn't take the hint though. The male roared as he charged at Obsidian, who waited, darting to the side as the male got in close. Unfortunately, he didn't get away with it this time. Two sets of claws raked across his side, slicing him open.

Obsidian snarled, seeing red. Bright, flashing red. Like a hundred neon signs in a small room. *Motherfucker!* He did a one-eighty, lashing out at Clay, who tumbled from the sky.

The male fell, head over tail, like a dragon snowball, down... down... down... Crashing hard into the ground below in a puff of sand. It was only then that he realized he had Clay's left wing hanging from his claw, which he was clutching tightly.

Oops!

Oh fuck!

Obsidian let the wing go, watching it fall, much in the same way the male had. It landed on the ground below, next to the downed male. And there it was, his own major weakness, at least when it came to training. He was strong and quick – and sometimes forgot how strong and how quick. Especially when instincts took over. Obsidian roared, feeling like a dick, but at the same time, justified. He had tried to go easy. Clay hadn't let him.

Without a backward glance, he headed for the skies. Mountain had been right. He needed to stay away. Demi was not his problem. If he was really honest with himself, as much as he wanted to believe otherwise, she never had been.

The cottage was spacious even though it didn't feel it right then. "We'd better get this over and done with."

Air… she needed air. "Get what over and done with?" Demi asked, knowing full well where he was going with this.

Cody looked angrier in that moment than she'd ever seen him before. "You know exactly what I'm talking about." He unbuttoned the top button of his pants. "We need to consummate this mating."

Demi gulped. "What?" she asked again, because she was obviously a sadist. Not just that. She was a hard of hearing sadist, just to make things worse.

"You heard me." Cody advanced on her.

"You can't be serious?" She took a step back.

He frowned. "Of course I'm serious. We just went through the whole mating ceremony. Everyone was there."

"I know," she half-yelled. "I'm not ready." She shook her head.

He narrowed his eyes. "That's bullshit, Demi!"

"I told you I didn't want this. I explained my feelings. I…"

"So, what?" He took another step towards her.

"I need to come to terms with this whole thing. With us." She worked hard at staying calm, at holding the last bit of ground she had.

"You've had six… make that, seven months to come to terms with this. I know it's difficult, but it's been long enough." He took another step. "We need to just bite the bullet, as the humans would say. It might not be as bad as you think. Hell, you might even enjoy it."

Enjoy it? No damned way. There wasn't much space left between them. "I wasn't prepared for today. I… need time. It's a big step. It's—"

"It's rutting." He shrugged. "Not a big deal, and as to time," he shook his head, a muscle in his jaw ticked, "you've had enough damn time," he growled.

This was Cody, she reminded herself. He wasn't going to hurt her. She knew him. Had known him her whole life. He was good, kind, smart. He was the male her sister had loved… adored.

"Why delay this any further?" he went on. "It has to happen. Surely you know that?"

"O-of course I do."

"No really?" He widened his eyes. Taking another step. It almost put them chest to chest at this point.

She put a hand on his chest and gave him a light shove. He didn't budge. "I mean, look at you… you're angry… you're…"

"Do you blame me, Demi?" he snorted out a laugh. "You cried throughout our entire mating ceremony. I had to keep reminding you where you were and what was happening. You barely listened to a word that elder said."

"I wasn't ready."

"You would never have been ready," his voice boomed,

and she flinched.

He sucked in a deep breath as he turned on his heel and headed for the other side of the room before spinning back. "Jesus! I won't hurt you. I would never force you to do anything."

"You forced this on me today. Where will it end?"

"I pushed you in the right direction, but I would never have forced you."

Like hell!

"As to forcing myself *on* you…" He shook his head. "No! It won't happen." He looked shocked she would even think such a thing.

"I know that," she whispered. "I know," she said again, more forcefully this time.

"You scent of another male," he growled. "Do you even know what that does to me, Brie?"

She choked out a sob.

Brie.

He'd called her by her dead sister's name. She was right… had been all along.

His eyes turned anguished. "I didn't mean that! Shit!" he growled the word. "I meant to say Demi. I… it… it was a mistake. I know who you are. I know exactly who you are." Cody walked back to her.

"Do you?" She swiped at a tear that tracked down her cheek.

"Of course," he growled.

"Because just yesterday you were telling me how I reminded you of her. I'm not Brie, I never will be. You can't use me to replace her. I know you loved my sister but… doing something like that won't work, Cody." She wiped away another tear. "And I think that's exactly what you're trying to do." She just needed to buy enough time to get him to see that.

"You do remind me of her, but I know you're not her." He pushed out a heavy breath. "I'll never get over Brie's death. I'll always blame myself for what happened." His throat worked, but that was it, he didn't show any more emotion.

Her tears came faster.

"But I *am* ready to move on," he insisted. "I do think this could work, I only wish you'd give us a chance."

She shook her head. Not convinced at all. "You are like a brother to me."

"Only I'm not, Demi." He lightly gripped her upper arms. "We don't share blood."

She looked into his familiar blue eyes. "We share Brie. The memory of her. If you had mated her, you would have become my brother. I can't let go of that either."

"Only, I didn't mate Brie. I mated *you.*"

Not yet! Not really! The thought rang through her mind like the ringing of a great bell. *Clang! Clang!*

He tried to cup her jaw, but she moved away. It was the intimacy the touch promised, that and the look in his eyes. It was too much. Pulling back wasn't even a conscious move. It just happened.

His eyes grew stormy, his brow creased. "You have three days to come to terms with this. You stink of that dragon at any rate. Once his scent has left you, we *are* making this official."

"Back to threatening me?" Her voice held an edge.

Cody made a noise of frustration. "You know what I mean."

Demi swallowed down her response. She didn't know what he meant. Who was this male? Cody had always been so sweet, so easygoing.

"Let's just hole up in here." He looked around them. "We can get to know each other."

Demi choked out a laugh. It held no humor. "I already know you. Your favorite color is green. You love fishing… in your skin… with rod and reel, like a human. You prefer sparring to running when in your fur and you… you loved my sister with all your heart." Her voice hitched. "You changed after she died. You changed after you became Alpha. You changed…" she whispered the last.

His chest heaved. The smile that had started to form on his lips died. His eyes welled up. "I guess we all changed," he shrugged. "How could we not? Three days, Demi." He held up three fingers. "We can't hide away from this. The elders… our fathers will lose their minds if they find out we haven't consummated this thing. They'll leave us alone, for now. Then…" He shrugged, making a noise of exasperation. "It will have to happen. Both packs will expect a proper union. You know that." He licked his lips. "And I want cubs. They'll have your olive skin and my light hair."

Oh god!

It was something he and Brie used to say all the time. It made her feel sick. Demi nodded anyway. A range of emotions that warred inside her. Everything from anger, to sorrow, to extreme guilt.

CHAPTER 11

Two days later…

The view of the valley was magnificent from up there, it didn't get too much better than this. Forests, streams, mountains in the distance. There was a herd of elk grazing upwind of him. The weather was mild, the wind ruffled his hair.

Obsidian stretched back against the cliff wall, the slate cool against his back. Yep… a magnificent view indeed. Especially since he could monitor all five paths that led away from Vale Creek. Away from the she-wolf's village.

He'd been able to stay away on day one. The day he'd torn off Clay's wing. Yesterday had been tough to get through though, and this morning had proven impossible. He'd tried to think about other things. Obsidian had gone hunting. He'd attended training but had been sent away on account of no one wanting to spar with him. He couldn't really blame them after Clay. Then here he was. He'd sort of just found himself there. Drawn to the place. Drawn to her. Another male's mate. His chest rumbled with the start of a low growl. He forced himself to look back upon that view. Hoping the vision before him was about to get better. Hoping a certain wolf would come into view. One with inky black fur and big dark eyes.

One with—*Wait... wait just a minute.* Movement. Up ahead. He squinted.

Fuck!

Not her. It wasn't Demi. He wanted to punch the cliff face. Remove chunks of rock. Smash and bash into it until his heartrate sped up to such a degree that his tension levels would go down.

He hadn't eaten much, or slept much, since leaving Demi in her back yard. Leaving her to her fate. He shouldn't have done it. He should have forced her to... Forced. *No, dammit!* If he forced her to do anything he'd be just as bad as her family. No, he'd made the right decision even if it still felt wrong. She'd needed him and he'd turned his back on her. Here he was, needing to see for himself one way or another. Mountain had tried to convince him she was just fine. Truth was though, that he'd feel wound up like this until he was sure.

He'd managed to capture a deer this morning. He'd been just about to sink his teeth into its soft fur, to tear its neck open but had stopped himself at the last second. Why kill it if he wasn't going to eat it? Even being in his scales wasn't as liberating. Hence why he was sitting there in his skin, just watching. Watching and waiting like an idiot.

His eyes tracked the lumbering bear as it picked up speed, running from the village like its ass was on fire. Too fast and agile to be a real bear. Too big as well. The creature must be a shifter. Someone from the village. Its fur was shaggy and thick. It was roughly one and a half times the size of Demi in her wolf form. Clearly male. The beast wasn't close enough for Obsidian to scent it, but he could see it was most likely the case. From its movements and his gut instinct, he was almost certain of that fact. He watched it lumber on, with waning interest. That was until the wind picked up again. The creature's scent hit him. It had him sitting straight up. Had his snout twitching. His scales sprouting. Obsidian leaped from the side of the cliff.

Her back prickled. Every hair on her body went up. Her blood flowed faster, rushing through her veins as her senses reached out, catching his heartbeat. The sound of his lungs filling. "You shouldn't sneak up on a person." She glanced back, quickly looking back down at the bread she was smearing with butter.

Shit! Shit! Shit!

It hadn't been three days yet. Today was day three. Technically she had until tomorrow. Not that it would matter. She'd still feel the same next week, next month, next year. She still wanted her allotted time though. Crazy as it sounded.

Why was he there? Dressed like that? With that look in his eyes? Demi was sure she could still scent Obsidian on herself. It was especially true since she hadn't used soap to wash. Bad but hey, she'd do whatever it took to avoid Cody. To avoid a moment like this, and so far it had worked. He had avoided her. Given her space. Allowed her to sleep in a separate bedroom. Was the reprieve over? She squeezed her eyes shut for a second before reaching for the sliced turkey.

"I was going to surprise you with lunch," he sounded

upbeat.

"Thanks, but," she shrugged, "I beat you to it." Her voice was a little shrill. "Do you want me to butter some bread for you?" She spoke too quickly.

"I… um… I could help."

"No… that's…"

He moved in next to her so Demi swallowed the rest of her words. He was wearing boxer shorts and nothing else. It made her feel uncomfortable. She realized that she'd put far too many turkey slices on her sandwich.

"Hungry?" Cody asked.

She could hear he was smiling but didn't want to make eye contact. "Um… yeah… I guess." She licked some of the mayonnaise off her finger.

"Looks good." Then his hand was on her back.

Shit!

Oh no!

"You just tensed up." He removed the hand.

She looked his way. "I'm… I…"

"You're not ready," he said it like an accusation.

"No! I'm not." She shook her head. Shook it hard. "You said three days." A stupid thing to say.

"Two days. Three days. What's the difference? Will you ever be ready? Is this a waste of time?"

"If I said yes, would it change anything?"

"No!" he snarled, his features softening almost immediately. "We are together now. We need to act like it." He put his hand on her arm.

"You're pushing me again." She knew she wasn't being fair but at the same time, she couldn't help her feelings. They weren't going to just change. Cody had forced this on her.

He'd used Obsidian to do it. Maybe it had just been desperation on his part, but she wasn't sure she could forgive him for that. "I don't like being pushed."

He folded his arms. "We said vows to one another."

"We said words, Cody. Only words."

He stepped away from her. "They were more than just words to me. I've waited years to say those words to..." He frowned.

"Years?" She shook her head, turning around to face him. "You keep catching yourself. I'm not Brie!"

"I know." Cody turned his attention to the food on the counter and threw the slices of bread on a plate. "I really do."

"I'm not really sure you do." She kept her eyes on him.

Cody remained impassive. He put down the knife he was holding and closed the distance between them, putting his hands on either side of her, trapping her against the counter. Her heart sped up and for all the wrong reasons.

"Your eyes have widened, and you scent of..." He sniffed. "Fear. You actually smell fearful. Are you afraid of me?"

"I don't know." She took a breath. "Should I be?"

"What kind of a question is that? You said it yourself, you know me. How can you be afraid of someone you have known your whole life?"

"I also said you had changed. The Cody I knew wouldn't..." She bit down on her lip.

"Wouldn't what?"

"Wouldn't be like this." She looked him up and down. At how his body caged hers. "So intimidating, so forceful... so manipulative."

"It's not like you left me much choice. You have no idea of the amount of pressure my father… both our fathers are putting on me. The elders in general." He took a step back and she could breathe.

"You're the Alpha. Ignore them."

"I can't! I can't ignore the wishes of our pack either. There is a lot on my plate and a lot at stake here. Do you even comprehend that?"

"I have an idea. This whole mating is a farce though, Cody. It's an unnecessary, outdated tradition."

"It's important to the packs. To our people."

"It isn't too late." There, she'd said it.

"Too late for what?" His eyes narrowed. The muscles on either side of his neck corded.

"Too late to stop this. To put an end to this madness. We could—"

He shook his head. "We went through with the ceremony."

She shrugged. "It doesn't matter. We can renounce our vows and go our separate ways."

"They may have been just words to you, but they meant something to me." He touched his chest. "We are together now. It's done! I *am* mating you, Demi. Deal with it! Tomorrow. Three days. We agreed."

"Actually, you dictated," she stated the facts.

"It's happening," he snarled. "Accept it or—"

"Or what?" She looked him head-on. It was her turn to narrow her eyes.

"Don't make me…"

"Make you what?" She definitely didn't know him anymore. How could a person change this drastically?

Cody growled, low and deep. His blue eyes glowing bright. His teeth were distinctly sharper. He took another step back. "I'm going now. I need to blow off some steam." She could see dark fur sprouting on his arms. Could see his muscles rope beneath his skin. He stormed from the room and she felt nothing but relief. What the hell was she going to do? There was no one she could talk to. Her family stood with Cody. Her best friend was gone. The funny thing was that Brie would have known what to do in this situation. She'd have had some bit of advice. Something simple and yet brilliant. Demi had no one left. No one on her side. She looked down at the sandwich, her appetite gone. Demi got to work packing everything away and wiping down the counter. She was in mid-wipe when there was a knock on the door. The back door.

She frowned.

CHAPTER 12

Obsidian knocked again, taking a couple of steps back. He didn't want to leave his scent on anything. Didn't want to get Demi into trouble.

He waited a whole minute. It felt more like an hour. Then he knocked again. "Demi," he whispered.

The door opened almost immediately. "Oh my god!" The she-wolf threw herself into his arms.

Obsidian caught her, wrapping his arms around her for a moment. She buried her face into his chest and held onto him. He breathed her in. It was as suspected, after catching the male's scent. "I thought you were mated. My brother must have..." he spoke under his breath, not wanting to alert anyone to his presence.

She tensed in his arms and pulled away. Her eyes were misty with emotion. "I am. I mean, I will be... I..." she floundered. Not making any sense.

"My brother said that you mated that male. It would have been two days ago now. That can't be though, since neither of your scents have changed." He sniffed. "In fact, I still scent myself on you. It's faint, but there." He frowned. "I came because I wanted to check that you were fine. I probably shouldn't have, but," he shrugged, "I couldn't get you off my mind. Mountain, my brother, he said you were fine and not my problem, but I feel differently."

"How did you know I was alone? That I was here in the first place, since I moved out of my old cottage?"

"I have been watching the village." He flinched. "I had to see that you were fine. I only came today, for the first time. I'm not some kind of freak. I'm worried, that's all."

"You were watching the village." She narrowed her eyes. "Now that really *is* stalker behavior." She folded her arms, pretending to be angry but he could see that she didn't mean it.

"I sat waiting for a couple of hours," he said. "Hoping to see you but instead, I saw your..." He couldn't say the word 'mate.' *Couldn't!* "I saw the bear," he grumbled. "I could scent it was him." His voice turned rasping and deep as he thought of the male.

"So you knew I would more than likely be alone?"

He nodded. "Dragons have an amazing sense of smell. I could smell you weren't where I left you. That you were here. I could hear that you were alone. I hope you don't think it's strange but... I've been worried about you. I could scent you weren't mated despite what Mountain told me. I needed to see you. To check in."

"Thank you for coming and for caring. It means so much, but," she shook her head, speaking quickly, "you have to go." She put her hands on his chest. She didn't push though. Just left them there.

Obsidian shook his head, taking in her beautiful dark eyes. Her hair was pulled into a messy ponytail. She wore jeans and a baggy t-shirt. "I should never have left you like that. Under those circumstances."

"Of course you should have," she spoke forcefully. "You would have been captured otherwise." She went back to whispering, looked around them, eyes wide. She took her hands back, leaving him feeling bereft without her touch. Obsidian could scent her pungent fear; it angered him to his core. "You still could be captured. If someone sees you, you'll be in trouble. Cody hates you. My father," she widened her eyes, "he was very upset when he found out what happened. He was almost more upset that it was consensual. He wanted you charged. Still does."

"With what?" Obsidian snorted. "I didn't do anything wrong. You didn't do anything wrong either."

"It doesn't matter. I did mate Cody two days ago," she blurted. Her body tensed and her already bloodshot eyes filled with tears. "It's done. I'm fine! You need to go."

Obsidian sniffed loudly, taking her scent in, keeping his eyes on her the whole time.

"I know." She licked her lips.

"You haven't consummated the mating. Why? Maybe because you don't love that male. I can see you're not fine. You haven't slept in days. You've been crying."

"Your brother is right. I'm not your problem. You can't get involved." There were dark smudges under her eyes as well and her frame wasn't as filled as it had been.

"It's too late for that."

"It's not." She looked around them some more, her voice animated, even though she was whispering. "You can leave and never look back. You have to do it."

It was exactly what he should do but he couldn't. The same drive that had made him come there in the first place was urging him to stay. Forcing him to try to fix it. "You scent of sorrow. Of guilt. Of pain." Those were some of the reasons he couldn't just up and leave her. "I see it. I feel it."

"It doesn't matter."

"It does to me."

Her face crumpled and tears ran down her cheeks. Obsidian put his arms around her. He had vowed he wouldn't touch so much as a hair on her head. Not wanting to leave his scent anywhere, but how could he not? She shook a little in his arms. She cried for a few seconds but soon pulled herself together. Demi pulled back, wiping her eyes and sniffing a few times. "I'm sorry. I need to stop crying. It doesn't help anything."

"Don't be sorry. You needed a shoulder. I happen to have a big one."

She laughed, still wiping at her tears. Her eyes were still filled with sadness. It was the scent of her fear that killed him though. It fucking killed him. It didn't take much for him to know exactly why she was afraid.

"Thank you!" she smiled – or tried to at any rate. "I feel so much better after seeing you, but you can't come again. I'm mated now… to Cody. This right now, seeing you, it's wrong."

"We're only talking. There's nothing wrong with that."

"I like you Obsidian. I like you a little too much. I think you're sweet and funny and really sexy. I can't see you again for all of those reasons. My future is with another male."

Her compliments made his heart beat faster. The rest of what she said, made him mad. "Are you sure there's nothing I can do to help you."

"Like what?"

He could only think of one thing. "Is Cody trying to

force… things?" He tried to put it as diplomatic as he knew how.

Her eyes darkened and she swallowed thickly. *Bingo!* He was right on the money.

She shook her head. "Cody is my mate. There is no such thing as forcing."

"Bullshit!" he all but snarled. "Besides, he isn't your mate yet and I'm guessing he's pushing to make that happen as soon as possible."

Her jaw tightened. "Wouldn't you?"

Obsidian shook his head and answered without hesitation. "No. That isn't a mating. It isn't a true partnership. It shouldn't be forced, it should just *be*. It's either there or it isn't. I wouldn't want to make that kind of commitment with someone who didn't love me back."

She looked wistful for a moment. "If only life was so uncomplicated."

"It shouldn't be this hard, Demi. It should be fun and exciting. Life should be an adventure. With the right person, it would be."

She chewed on her lower lip, her eyes welling again. "You're right. Sometimes though, we need to accept what we are dealt and make the most of it. I'm fine! Thank you for caring." She took his hand and squeezed it. "Like I said before, you have no idea what it means to me. You need to go now though. No one can see you and you can't come back. Promise me." She squeezed his hand a second time. "I'm worried about you."

Obsidian shook his head. "I can't promise that, and I'm more worried about you."

She laughed. It lasted all of a few seconds, but it was the best sound in the world. "Look at us. Listen to us. I meant it though." She sighed. "I don't mean to be ungrateful."

"When I'm convinced you're safe. That you're happy. I'll stay away, but until then," he squeezed her hand back, loving the feel of her soft skin, "you're stuck with me." This female clearly didn't have anyone else in her corner.

She smiled, letting his hand go. "Okay. The only reason I'm agreeing is because I suspect I don't have much of a choice."

"In this one thing... no," he shook his head, "but in all others, you will always have a choice with me. I would never take that basic right away from you." He burned with anger. It churned in his gut. "I'm going to leave now but I will be back. That male can't force you to do anything you're not ready for. Don't let him or anyone else convince you otherwise. It doesn't matter that you were promised to that bear. It doesn't matter that you went through with the mating ceremony. All of that is ultimately bullshit."

She nodded. "I know." She looked shocked. "I agree wholeheartedly."

"Okay then. Take care of yourself." He pulled her into a quick one-armed hug. Not wanting to cross any lines even though he was tempted to obliterate them.

"You too. Be careful when you leave. Don't let anyone see you and whatever you do, don't get caught."

"I won't." Get caught that was. Being seen though. That might be difficult with what he had planned.

The male ground to a halt, his paws digging into the earth. He snarled, his eyes narrowing on Obsidian who had shifted into his skin. He folded his arms, not worried. He could take this fucker in human form. No problem.

The bear circled him, it had icy blue eyes, making him look freaky. It happened with shifters sometimes though. Those eyes were narrowed on him and filled with hate. His lip curled from his teeth in a silent growl.

"We need to talk," Obsidian said, ignoring the antics.

The bear circled the other way. This time he did growl, low and deep. His teeth exposed, saliva dripped onto the earth. The bear crouched, looking like he might pounce at any moment. "You and I both know I can take you, even with one arm tied behind my back," Obsidian stated the facts. "You might be the strongest shifter in your pack, but you're no match for a dragon. Let's talk male to male and then I'll let you go."

Cody growled again, putting everything in it. The bear looked agitated and pissed off. Obsidian didn't give a shit.

A few seconds went by before he finally shifted. Obsidian watched as its fur pulled back. Same with its jaw, snout, ears and teeth. Until a male stood before him, chest heaving. Sweat on his brow and death in his eyes. "What the fuck are you doing here? On our territory uninvited? You are trespassing. I could throw you in a cage just for being here, let alone," he narrowed his eyes, "for rutting my female."

"She was hardly yours," Obsidian said, staying calm.

"She is now!" he spat.

"That's why I'm here."

The male's nose twitched. "I can scent her on you. You went to see her! You have no right to go anywhere near her, dragon. I could call for your balls."

"But you won't," Obsidian said. "I'll deny it and Demi will back me up. We both know that. You can scent that nothing happened between us."

Cody shook his head, looking disgusted.

"The only reason I came back was to check in on Demi… as a friend. I wanted to make sure she was okay."

"Well, you can fuck off now. She's fine. We're mated!"

"She's sad."

Cody shook his head. "We all have our problems. She will get used to things as they are."

"She's unhappy."

"She won't be for long," the bear insisted.

"She's afraid… *of you*. Did you know that?"

He looked unsure for a spilt second before schooling his emotions. "She has nothing to be afraid of. She's mine to protect. I will look after Demi. I would give my own life for her."

"Protect her?" Obsidian asked, raising his brows.

"Yes, dammit!" the bear snarled.

"Even from yourself?"

He frowned. "What bullshit are you talking about?"

"You know exactly what I'm talking about. Are you going to force her to consummate this union?"

His jaw tightened. "It needs to happen."

"That's a yes then," Obsidian snarled. "You'll rape your own female. Is that what you're saying?"

"No! Fuck no!" Cody yelled. "Are you crazy? This has fuck all to do with you anyway. It's none of your business."

"I'm making it my business, bear. If you hurt her…" He got in the male's face. Right up in there. "If you force her to do anything… I'll kill you. It would mean a death sentence for me, but I'd gladly take it." He smiled.

"For a female you don't even know?" The bear looked like he didn't buy it.

"Yes. She's a good female. Demi is kind, beautiful and

sweet. She doesn't deserve this. No one does. Her sadness resonates with me in a way you will never understand." Obsidian had felt alone for longer than he could remember.

"We belong together. Not that it's any of your business, but I love her." His expression clouded. It made Obsidian think that maybe the male meant it. It helped him breathe a little easier. It also made his chest feel tighter. Cody narrowed his eyes. "I would never hurt her in that way. Now," he poked at Obsidian's chest, "you need to back the fuck off. You need to leave her alone. Leave *us* alone. She will struggle to commit if you keep sniffing around." There was a growl to his voice.

"I will be back bear. I *will* check up on Demi. Once I'm satisfied she isn't in any danger, I'll leave you alone. Then and only then."

"She's mine," Cody snarled, his face inches from Obsidian's.

"Don't hurt her and we'll be just fine," he warned. "Forcing her to do anything else she doesn't want to do would be hurting in my opinion."

"Stay the fuck away!" the bear spoke softly, eyes blazing. "You'll regret it if you don't."

"Treat her with respect. Trust me," Obsidian narrowed his eyes, "you won't live to regret it if you don't."

"Are you threatening me?"

The bear was slow-witted. Obsidian nodded. "Most definitely."

"Does Demi know you are here? Did she put you up to this?"

"No! This is between me and you, bear. Don't push me or—"

"For the last time, she's mine. Demi is mine! It's a matter

of time before it is made official. I won't need to force her. Do you hear that, dragon? She'll crouch down onto all fours for *me*. She'll scream *my* name. Bear my young. *Mine!*"

Obsidian was panting. Working hard at keeping his rage in check. Only because this male was right. Everything he was saying was correct. As much as he wanted to break every bone in his body, he couldn't. "Then we have nothing to worry about. I will be back. I will be watching."

Obsidian shifted in two seconds flat. He was above the clouds in under three. He needed to keep in mind that Demi belonged to someone else. Once he knew she was safe, he needed to stay away from Vale Creek.

CHAPTER 13

Two days later…

Demi sat up, the sheets were tangled around her body. She was panting heavily, her brow felt sweaty. Her throat felt like it was closing. She clutched a hand to her chest, trying to calm down. Trying to get air into her lungs.

Her sister's anguished screams still rang in her ears. One minute she and Cody had been so happy and the next… death and destruction. Then there was the laughing. That godawful laughing. She knew that part wasn't real. Why did she keep hearing it?

"What is it?" Cody called from the doorway. His hair was mussed, his eyes bleary with sleep.

"Um…" She struggled to catch her breath. To think clearly.

"Was it that nightmare you keep having?" he asked, coming into her room. "The one you have every night?" He rubbed his eyes. "Tonight sounded worse than normal."

Shoot! He had obviously heard her before. It wasn't normally this bad though. Maybe she'd shouted out in her sleep or something. She nodded once.

"Do you want to talk about it?" He sat on the edge of her bed.

"I'm fine." She pulled some of her hair behind her ear. Her breathing was normal. Her heartrate too.

"Talking will help." He touched the side of her arm. "I could bring you some warm milk or," he shrugged, "a hot chocolate or something."

"I dream about the same thing every night." She licked her lips and then rubbed a hand over her face. "I dream about her death."

His face grew pinched. "Brie's death?"

She nodded. "I dream about the accident. It's like I'm there but I can't do anything to stop it." She left it at that. She couldn't tell him about the laughing.

"You have the same nightmare every night?"

She nodded again. "I don't know why, and I can't get it to stop." The only peaceful sleep she had managed to steal was in Obsidian's arms. In over a year, that was it. "It's the same every time. At first, the two of you are so happy. You're talking and laughing and then... then..." her lip quivered, "the accident happens," she stated simply.

His eyes softened. "That's terrible. No wonder you're having such a hard time. Come here." He opened his arms, looking very much like the Cody she remembered. The male she liked.

Demi let him hug her. He held her tightly at first, then eased his hold.

This was okay.

This was fine.

She needed to allow this. Had to... He rubbed her back softly, in lazy circles designed to soothe.

See.

It was still okay.

Fine.

No worries.

Then she heard him sniffing softly, his face lightly touching her head. *Holy shit!* He was sniffing her. *No! Please stop!* This was bad. Very bad.

"Don't tense up, Demi, please," he asked.

"I can't help it. You're..."

"Scenting you," Cody stated. He still held her. "Yeah, I am."

When a male scented a female, it was to initiate sex. "I just had a nightmare and you're scenting me," she sounded incredulous. Who could blame her?

"I know that and, for the record, I'm not trying to be insensitive. I want to help you forget... at least for a little while." He kissed her on the top of her head. "Please let me..."

She pulled away, shaking her head.

"Lie back. Close your eyes." He crouched over her, his arms on either side of her.

"You're caging me in again." Her heart pounded.

"I won't hurt you. I swear. I just want to touch you... hold you. I just want you." He leaned in, kissing her neck. "Need you," he murmured.

"I'll take hot chocolate," she blurted, voice shrill, trying to shrink away.

Cody tensed as he pulled away. He sighed. "At least let me ease you. No rutting... not yet at any rate."

Not yet.

Ease.

His touch felt all wrong. Everything about it. *Wrong! Wrong! Wrong!* "Please." She sucked in a deep breath. "I can't."

He pulled himself up, holding himself over her with his arms. "We can't keep avoiding this, Demi. At least, let me kiss you." His gaze drifted to her lips. "We have to start somewhere."

Cody was right. They needed to, at least, try. She needed to try. They had to move forward at some point. Even if it felt like she was committing a sin. Maybe if she allowed the kiss, he would leave her alone. Obsidian was going to come back and maybe he would end up getting caught this time. Cody was her mate now. It didn't matter how wrong it felt. This needed to happen. Demi nodded once.

Cody lowered himself slowly. Demi closed her eyes. He slanted his lips over hers. She felt his tongue and almost freaked out. "I can't!" she blurted, turning her head to the side. She may as well kiss Serge.

The bed shook as he stood up. "Why not?" His voice was animated. His eyes blazed. "And don't give me some bullshit about still seeing me as a brother."

"More like an asshole," she countered, pulling the blanket more securely around her.

"We can't hide out for much longer," he snapped back. "I'll be the laughing stock of both packs if anyone finds out we haven't rutted."

"I don't care what everyone thinks. Let them think whatever they want. It shouldn't matter!"

"It does matter," he growled. "I am the goddamned Alpha. How will anyone respect me? I can't even get my own mate to accept me."

"You should have thought of that before you forced me into this farce of a mating," she snapped. Demi had never minced her words about how she felt. She wasn't about to start now.

"No one forced you. You walked down that aisle of your own accord. There was no sliver-bladed sword to your heart."

She couldn't believe what she was hearing. "There may as well have been. You threatened Obsidian. He would've been in a silver cage by now if I hadn't done it. I warned you, Cody. I don't love you in that way and I never will. I thought I could find a way to push past that fact, but I can't!"

"You haven't given it a chance. It's that blasted dragon again! I am so over that fucker. If it weren't for him, we'd be fine."

"No, we wouldn't!"

"Yes, we would. You developed feelings for him. You would have accepted me by now if it weren't for him. Admit it!"

"I'll admit that I was… *am* attracted to him. I will never feel that way about you even though you are an attractive male. I just don't! It's how it is. He isn't holding me back though." She shook her head. "That isn't it at all."

"I don't believe you, Demi." His eyes were narrowed on hers. For a second there, her breath caught in her lungs. The way he was looking at her, his words, it was like Cody knew Obsidian had been to see her. She'd taken a long bath. Had washed herself from head to toe with berry-scented soap. He hadn't said anything to her when he'd returned two and a half hours later. No, there was no way he could know. He would never keep quiet if he had somehow found out about it. He walked back over to her, pushing her back on the bed. Her back hit the mattress with a light thud. He was on her in a second, straddling her thighs and holding her hands above her head. His penetrating stare on hers.

"Cody," she struggled against him, "what the hell!"

"Kiss me!" he demanded through clenched teeth. "Just do it. I'm not so bad. It won't be as terrible as you think."

"Let me go!" She tried to yank free. "What has gotten into you?" she yelled. "What the hell is wrong with you?"

"Kiss me!" he growled again, sounding desperate. "I'm your mate and you can't even kiss me." He finally let her go.

Her heart was racing. She struggled to catch her breath.

"I swear, Demi, you need to accept this. You're forcing my hand here. I don't want to have to…" Cody shook his head once instead of finishing the sentence. His chest heaved. His eyes were filled with… *rage*… pure and simple.

"What happened to you Cody? Why are you like this?"

"Nothing happened," he all but snarled. "I have accepted this. I've accepted us. You need to do the same."

"Or what? You're not saying it, but I can hear it."

"You don't want to find out, Demi. You need to get your mind right. I've tried being your friend. I've tried giving you space. What do you want? Dinner? Long walks in the forest? I'll light candles. Sprinkle rose petals. I'll do anything you want, but this needs to happen, and it needs to happen soon."

"I still hear an 'or else' in there and I don't like it."

"Damn straight there's an 'or else,'" he snarled. "I've tried being nice and I'm starting to struggle with it."

"More threats. What will it be this time?" She sounded defeated. "There is nothing more you could possibly take away from me."

"You make it sound like being with me is akin to a death sentence."

"You were a good male but I'm not sure anymore. It's how I feel right now. How you're making me feel. Stop caring so much about what others think and – for claw's sake – stop with the threats already."

"It seems like threats are the only thing that work with you. This can go two ways. You are going to be the decider." He pointed at her. His chest heaved a few times before his whole demeanor softened. "Please, Demi. I beg you. Please. I'll get on my knees if I have to. Tell me what you want from me to help you accept this."

He was giving her whiplash. One second a total asshole and the next the nice guy she had always known. "There is nothing you can do. This whole thing was a mistake. I mated you to protect Obsidian. I hoped you would come to your senses but you're getting worse."

"You have to at least try to make this work."

"I did." Tears streamed down her face. "It may not seem that way to you, but I really did. I can't be with you in that way and I need you to leave now," she whispered the last. "You're not making sense. You're not yourself right now. I'm worried about you, Cody. You're doing this for all the wrong reasons."

"I'm fine!" his voice boomed. "It's you who has the problem. That problem is the dragon!" he snarled. "That fucking beast," he muttered, as he left the room, slamming the door behind him.

She was going to speak with her father in the morning. Demi hoped and prayed that for once, just for once, he would listen. That he would stop being a Council member and just be her father.

CHAPTER 14

The next day…

"WW here are you going?" Mountain folded his arms, leaning against the edge of the balcony. The cliffs and vast ocean behind him.

Obsidian grunted. *Shit!* For a second there, he thought he had gotten away without being seen. Mountain had been keeping tabs on him. He'd been using Shale and Stone as well. Today, it was him personally. *What a ballache!*

"No way." His brother shook his head. "Grunting isn't going to work on me. Not anymore. You've been talking just fine. Where are you headed? One of the males mentioned that you scented of a female yesterday. That the scent was musky… wolf-like."

"He was mistaken," Obsidian countered. His voice a rough rasp.

"What are you playing at?"

"Playing?" He snorted, shaking his head. "I'm not into games."

Mountain narrowed his eyes. "What the fuck are you doing?"

"Nothing that concerns you."

"Your safety and wellbeing concern me plenty. I told Stone that you would be at training later today. You should try to focus on other things. Take your mind off of a certain female."

Obsidian chuckled. "Training, you say? What would be the point? After de-winging that asshole, Clay, no one will go against me." He snorted. "The fucker was antagonizing me. It was only one measly wing. You would think I beheaded the male."

Mountain laughed. "I wish I had been there to see you rip his wing off."

"Bull!" Obsidian rubbed his chin. "You had better things to do. You were with your mate."

"You are right," Mountain nodded. "I can have a word with the males. I… I'll make sure they allow you to train with them again. You are an asset to us. Or, at least, you could be."

"Thank you, but no." Obsidian shook his head. "Don't bother. I'm going to do some border patrol… alone. I need some time to myself." His voice was becoming corded as he started to shift.

Mountain put a hand on his shoulder. "Stay away from her, brother. It can only end in heartache. Please!"

"I can look after myself."

"Don't do it." Mountain was frowning.

"Demi has no one," Obsidian pushed the words out between clenched teeth.

"She has her mate."

Mate.

Right.

"The male is unstable. I don't like the way he treats her. He's a prick!" Obsidian growled.

"None of our business. Why am I having to repeat myself? Stay the fuck away from her." His demeanor softened some. "I don't want you killed."

Obsidian choked out a laugh. "Let them try. As soon as I am sure she is safe… I will…"

"Fuck! I had hoped I was reading this wrong. You've already been, haven't you? That male did scent wolf on you?"

"Yes, they haven't consummated the mating yet. That bear fucker is trying to force her. If he does…" Obsidian shook his head. "If he…"

"What?"

"I'll kill him," Obsidian snarled.

"Then both of you will lose your lives. You know that, don't you? You'll be put to death with his blood on your hands." Mountain gripped both his biceps. "You have to reconsider."

"In that case, it will have been worth it. I need to make sure that he does right by her. Once I'm convinced, I'll stay away." Obsidian narrowed his eyes on Mountain's. "I swear."

"He'll never do right by her. Not in your eyes. You're biased. You have feelings for this female. I can tell. This protective behavior. It can only end in heartache since she has a male already."

"I will keep that in mind." Obsidian's heart pounded.

"Will you?"

"Yes!"

"I don't think you can do that."

"I will!" he countered. "Demi has made it clear that she has no choice but to stay with this prick."

"Her mate."

Obsidian clenched his jaw. *Not yet he wasn't! Fuck!* Was he doing this to try to stop them from consummating the union?

It didn't matter. Either way, Demi needed protecting. He was going to be the one to do it since no one else would.

"Take care, brother," he heard Mountain say, his voice full of emotion.

Obsidian completed his shift. Then he took to the skies and headed for Demi's village, staying high so that he wouldn't be easily spotted. He flew straight to the cottage, circling a couple of times.

One heartbeat.

Just the one.

Unfortunately, he was too high to be able to tell whether it was the bear or Demi who was home. He scanned the area. Thankfully, the cottage was on the outskirts of town, bordering on the forest. He couldn't see anything, or anyone, so he decided to move in closer. This was risky. He realized that. Probably stupid but he had to be sure that Demi was still okay.

Obsidian dropped quickly. If someone happened to be looking just then, they might see something, but he'd be gone so quickly that they'd second guess themselves. They couldn't see him so high up and they couldn't see him once he touched down. It was that split-second in-between that he was vulnerable. Drifting down slowly was not an option, so speed and stealth were his friends.

He touched down noiselessly in the back yard, taking in a snoutful of air. *The bear! Damn!* He listened for movement. For a change in the rhythm of the male's heartbeat just to make sure he hadn't been spotted. It carried on rhythmically. In fact, he'd wager that the male was probably sleeping based on the fact that it was slow and steady.

Demi wasn't there. Didn't matter, he'd hit the clouds and keep a look out for her. Obsidian wasn't going to approach her though, unless her prick-of-a-mate had hurt her in any way. Then he'd be forced to kill the fucker. He'd take whatever was dealt to him. No problem!

He was just crouching down to take off when something hit him in the chest. It was instantly hard to breathe. It stung. His mouth fell open. *What?*

Obsidian flapped his wings a couple of times, his body lifting but it felt heavy. Something else hit him, also in the chest, making him grunt this time. His limbs felt like they were suddenly made from lead. He was gasping for air, but it didn't seem to reach his lungs, which felt like they were on fire.

Obsidian crashed back down to the earth even though he was only a few feet in the air. He fell over onto his side and coughed. Blood bubbled up into his mouth.

Blood?

What?

Why?

His vision was turning hazy. He…

"I told you to stay away." The bear looked down at him. It took him a while to focus on what was in his hand. A bow. Strapped to the male's back was a quiver, with green-feathered arrows sticking out of the top. He looked down to where four of them stuck out from his chest.

Four?

He'd only felt two. From the way his chest was burning, they had to be silver. He was so fucked! Obsidian coughed up a spray of blood. Then he blacked out.

CHAPTER 15

The backpack fell to the ground as Demi shifted into her human form. She took out her clothing and quickly got dressed. Next, she slipped on her sneakers before heading up the path that led to the front door of her parents' house.

She knocked once, stepping back. It didn't take long for her mom to open up. Her face instantly brightened. "Sweetie, what a fantastic surprise. I didn't expect to see you for another day or two. Where's Cody?" She looked past Demi, down the path.

"Hey, mom." She smiled as her mom's eyes moved back to lock with hers. "It's just me."

"I see. Come on in." Her mom gestured inside the house and then pulled her into a tight hug as soon as she was inside.

"Please don't say anything." Demi knew her mother would be able to scent that she and Cody hadn't consummated their mating yet.

"I wouldn't dream of it," her mom said, squeezing her arms. Demi noticed that she looked really tired. "You don't have to do anything you don't want to do."

"Too late for that," Demi muttered, wishing she hadn't when she saw her mom's eyes cloud over.

"You know what I mean. Don't take the next step until you are absolutely ready. You need to know, by the way, that I'm against this whole thing." That came as a shock. It was the first time her mom had done anything other than encourage a relationship with Cody. "I don't like the way it's been handled. I—"

"Demi." Her father rounded the corner. "I *thought* I heard you two talking."

Demi noticed how her mother's back went stiff. How she set her jaw as soon as her eyes landed on her father. Her dad was looking her way. He frowned, his nostrils flaring.

"I came to see you about something," she quickly blurted, not wanting to cause any more trouble between her parents, because there was clearly trouble brewing.

Her dad nodded. "Let's go into my study to talk then."

"Would you like something to drink, honey?" her mom asked.

"I'm fine, thanks," her dad responded.

"I was talking to Demi." Her mom's tone was distinctly cold.

"Um… I'm fine, thanks, mom." She looked between her parents. Maybe she shouldn't have come. Then again, she was there now, may as well get it over with.

"Anytime, sweetie." Her mom hugged her again. "I know you moved out a few years ago already, but I wanted you to know that this is still your home."

"Demi has a home and a life of her own," her father said.

"Don't butt in," her mom kept her eyes on her, "I mean it," she added. "I love you so much." Her eyes shone with sincerity. "I'm sorry I haven't been there for you. I've been so focused on what I lost, I forgot to recognize what was still right in front of me. I'm with you on this…"

"Delila," her father warned.

"Don't you Delila me!" her mother yelled.

"Thank you, mama," Demi said, trying to defuse the situation. She felt something ease in her. This despite the friction in the room. "I appreciate it. I need to talk with dad about a couple of things."

"I mean it." Her mom gripped her by the hand and squeezed.

"I know you do, and I love you too." She squeezed back before letting go. Her mother nodded once, her demeanor relaxing slightly.

They made their way to his study. "You're not mated yet," her father stated, as soon as the door was closed.

Talk about getting right down to business. "I'm fine thanks, and you?"

"This is serious, Demi. There have been fights within the packs. Why haven't you mated yet? Why are you putting off the inevitable?"

"I told you that I don't love him."

"Do you think that every female for generations has been in love with her promised and vice versa? I'll answer for you, Demi, it's a no. A resounding no. Of course not. Everyone has done their bit. Your mom and I had it hard to begin with, but we made it work. We all did our part. You need to do yours."

"We live in the twenty-first century now, dad. It's no longer the dark ages. You had it happen to you. You know how it feels. It's an outdated tradition."

"You're sounding like a human. We're not humans. We

are governed so much more by our traditions, our heritage. Not loving him isn't enough to not go through with this. You need to do this. I know Cody is on board. Please, honey." His shoulders slumped and he rubbed his eyes, looking stressed and tired. There was more grey in his hair and crow's feet around his eyes. His skin looked sallow. Guilt flared.

"Cody isn't acting like himself though, dad. I'm worried about him."

"Take a seat." He gestured to a chair on the other side of his desk. He himself moved around it and sat down, leaning back and folding his hands. "Tell me everything."

She went on to tell her father how Cody had manipulated her using Obsidian. About what had happened the night before, how Cody had held her down and tried to kiss her. "The worst of it is that he has called me Brie a couple of times. I suspect he's going to use me as a replacement for her. So, not only do I feel like I'm betraying my sister, I'm doing it with a male who is pretending I'm her. It makes it so much worse."

"That may be true," her father shrugged, "but it is still no reason to call off the mating."

"No reason? You can't mean that!"

"I do." He nodded. "Cody is trying to do his best to make the most of a difficult situation. He is under a lot of pressure."

"He's doing his best to accept this by pretending I'm Brie."

He raised his brows. "If that's what it takes."

Demi couldn't believe what she was hearing. "I don't think he's worked through his grief. We've never once seen him break down over Brie's passing. Think about it. Sure, he's been upset about it. Riddled with guilt because he blames himself, but he's never actually grieved. The only time he visited the burial grounds was when we..." She paused a second, feeling her chest tighten to the point of pain. "Was for the passing ceremony."

Her father shrugged. "Cody is a male. He will have grieved in his own time. In his own way."

"I think you're wrong, dad. You haven't spent any time with him lately. It's more than anything he has said or done. It's a feeling I have. It's how he is making me feel. The Cody I've always known is kind and sweet. This new Cody, Alpha Cody, he's forceful, angry and manipulative. He's desperate to make this happen and I don't think he's doing it for the reasons you think. He used what happened with the dragon..."

Her father slapped the table. "It was Cody who insisted we leave the beast be."

"What?" She lifted her brows, not quite believing what she was hearing.

"Laird and I wanted retribution. That beast should never have been on our territory in the first place. If the thing had stayed on its side of the line, what happened, would never have transpired." He shook his head. "It's put a rift between you and Cody... your mate, for fur's sake!"

"That's nonsense!" She stood up. "Cody protected Obsidian but only so that he could use him as a pawn. That's it! What happened with Obsidian was a direct reflection of my feelings. My pent-up emotions. My resentment of what I was being coerced into doing on the basis of tradition." She kept her eyes on her father, feeling instantly bad. Although Obsidian had been a quick rut – a means to an end – he had meant so much more as well. "Don't blame the dragon. I seduced him. I wanted him— "

"That beast should never have been here. What happened, happened. It's done! Just like your mating. It is done!" He sucked in a deep breath. "Please sit down." He gestured to the chair behind her. "I told you this because I want you to stop blaming Cody. I think it's commendable how he's taken everything in his stride. How he was willing to look past your indiscretion."

Commendable!

Indiscretion?

She collapsed back into the chair. "What indiscretion? I never agreed to anything prior to Obsidian. Everyone keeps acting like I did this terrible thing. Well, I didn't!"

"You became Cody's promised the day we buried," he cleared his throat, "Brie."

"Listen to yourself!"

"Let's not argue about this." He kept his eyes on her. "All we do lately is argue."

It was true. They were never going to see eye to eye on this. There was no point in arguing anymore. They both recognized that fact. She nodded once.

"Cody is still the male you remember, only, he's in a difficult place. His instincts will be up and in full force. Instincts telling him to finish the mating. I can't imagine how he's coping." Her father looked concerned. More concerned about Cody than his own daughter. It hurt.

"He doesn't want to finish the mating with me. He wants Brie. Dad, I can't go through with it."

"It's too late, Demi. You *are* mated!"

"I'm not though! Not really. Please, dad. Please talk to Laird. He's your best friend for claw's sake. Maybe he can talk some sense into his son. Cody might listen to him. Why do we need to follow these traditions? I don't get it. We can all still walk away. Both Cody and I will have a shot at being happy. Despite what Cody says, he *doesn't* want me. He *doesn't* love me and will *never* be happy if we are forced to mate."

"Don't even go there. I can't discuss this with Laird."

"Can't or won't?"

"That's just it!" Her father shook his head. "Laird and I are not on great terms anymore."

She frowned. "You've been best friends forever though."

"He was angry when you… disappeared that night. We haven't seen eye to eye on a couple of things lately. Our relationship is… strained. It's a good reflection of what's happening between the packs."

Demi was shocked at the admission. Her father and Cody's dad had been the best of friends ever since she could remember. The packs were fine, weren't they? It was probably her father trying to get her to finish the mating. "Talk to Cody, then. You do it!" Even though she knew this conversation was futile, she needed to try one last time.

Her dad leaned forward, resting his arms on the desk in front of him. "I can't do that. It would cause further discord. I'll say it again, what is happening between Laird and me is proof that the two packs are not necessarily as close as you think. That bonds are not as tight. It is not a chance I am prepared to take."

"Even for me?" It was a question she hadn't asked. All this time, and she'd held back pushing this far.

He swiped a hand over his face. "As the ex-Alpha, as one of the Council members, I have to think of our people. Of the wolves. We are outnumbered by the bears, who are stronger. We would be crushed if there was ever a war. You need to mate Cody."

It was like a slap across the face… a blade to the heart.

"I'm sorry, Demi. If things could be different…"

There was a great commotion outside. Yelling, snarling… many footfalls. More yelling. Her mother burst into the study. "They are saying that dragon has been captured. That Cody took it down…" Her eyes moved to Demi. "I'm sorry, honey. It looks like the beast has been gravely injured."

The blood drained from her body.

CHAPTER 16

Demi stood there with her hands over her mouth. Her body felt cold.

Obsidian lay on his back. His chest rose and fell in quick succession. He wheezed and gasped as he struggled to breathe. There were holes in his chest. They oozed blood. One… two… three… four of them.

Good lord! A burst of adrenaline hit her system. *Obsidian is still alive,* she told herself. Still breathing. Still here. It meant that he would recover. She could breathe a little easier. At least for the time being.

She took in Cody and the four bloody arrows in his blood-smeared hands. She fought to school her emotions. Demi couldn't give away how much this affected her. Right then, she wished with all her heart that she had taken Obsidian up on his offer. "What have you done?" she asked, as Cody shut the door to the cage. "Have you gone mad?" she kept her voice level. "The dragons are going to wage a war on us after this."

"You can all leave now. Brutus and Max, the two of you

can wait outside. I need to speak with my female."

"Hardly yours," one of the males muttered.

"What was that?" Cody snarled, turning towards the males. His free hand curling into a fist. His muscles strained.

No one said anything. She scented fear.

"Get out of here!" Cody snapped at the males, who were still milling about. They all hustled outside. The door closed with a sharp click that reverberated around the room.

"He was in our back yard, Demi. I told him not to come back and yet here he is. The dragons won't have a leg to stand on in this case. I warned him twice and—"

"Twice?" Her heart began to pound.

"Yes, twice. I know he was here yesterday. That he came to see you. What you don't know is that he came to see me too. That beast threatened me." His eyes shone brightly.

The blood returned to her body in a flood. Heat crept up from under her collar. "Why didn't you say anything?" She didn't wait for a response. "Wait a minute! That's why you acted the way you did." She squeezed her eyes shut for a second. "It makes more sense now."

"I acted the way I did because you insist on standing in our way. I warned you about that as well. I knew he would come back. I didn't think he'd make it quite so easy for me to catch him though." Cody smiled. It was cold and calculating.

"You planned this?" There was a shrillness to her voice.

"I fetched the bow and arrows from the weapons room before returning home from my run yesterday. Run." He snorted. "My run-*in* is a more apt description. I don't like being threatened." He shook his head.

"So, you fetched silver weapons, like a coward?" Anger bubbled inside her. "You set a trap."

"You left me with little choice. I won't stand for a dragon sniffing around my female... my mate. I hadn't planned anything yet." He shrugged. "But the opportunity arose, and I took it."

"But you ultimately planned on hurting Obsidian... on capturing him?"

"Yes." Cody nodded. Zero hesitation. In fact, he looked smug. "You can't blame me, Demi. You are *mine*," he snarled, "and yet the dragon won't stay the fuck away and you won't... let me anywhere near you. There is a correlation between the two."

"Nothing happened yesterday between Obsidian and me," she spat. "The only correlation is you acting like a crazy person and the fact still remains that we don't love each other. You're trying to use me to replace Brie."

"No." He shook his head. "That's not it at all." He didn't put much into the argument, even looked like she might have hit a nerve.

"You've never fully accepted Brie's death. You don't like to talk about it. You've never grieved. *Never.* It isn't right, Cody."

"I said that wasn't it," he growled. "Leave it be. We can't move forward if we keep looking back and we certainly can't move forward until the dragon is out of our lives once and for all."

"What are you saying?" Fear hit. "What are you going to do to him?"

"That all depends on you." He folded his arms. "We need to decide what happens to the beast. I can put this to Council, or as Alpha, I can make a decision myself."

Shit!

Terrible options. Cody hated Obsidian. Her father too.

Her father trusted Cody. One thing she knew though was that as one of the Council members, her father wouldn't go easy on Obsidian. Neither would Laird. They were both highly influential members of the Council. Obsidian was in a world of trouble and all because of her.

"Your father wants it put down," Cody said. "He believes the dragon took advantage of you while you were in a vulnerable state. He doesn't believe the rutting was fully consensual. My father is in agreement."

"That's bullshit and you know it!" she yelled.

"Do I?" Cody asked.

She growled in frustration. "You know full well—"

"I am going to make your father aware of the threats made to my life as well. This is the third time the dragon was trespassing on our territory. All in all, we have a good case to take its head."

"No!" she shouted. "How can you even—"

"That's the way this will go down, but only if I decide to put this decision to Council." He paused, letting his statement sink in.

Demi could hardly breathe. She could hardly think, her heart was beating so hard and so loudly.

"If I were to make the decision as Alpha, I could make sure that things go down differently. I would ensure his release. Maybe a lighter sentence…" He pretended to think it through. Again, everything about this was calculated. "Death would be off the table. Maybe fifty lashes…" He shrugged. "I'd have to think about it."

"You nearly killed Obsidian!" she shouted. "How could you possibly want to beat him as well? Please, Cody, I know you're hurting over Brie, over what happened but— "

His face morphed with pain. Just a second and then it was

gone. "Stop bringing Brie into this. It has nothing to do with her... or what happened. You need to make a decision. The clock is ticking."

Demi turned back to Obsidian. She gripped the bars but recoiled when her hands burned.

"Careful," Cody warned unnecessarily. "They're silver."

She rubbed her hands together as the burn faded.

"Let's finish the mating and I swear I'll make sure the dragon is released. Once we are mates, he'll have no more reason to keep coming onto our lands. I'll spend the rest of my life proving to you that I'm worthy. Believe it or not, I don't want to see him killed." Cody looked into the cage. "I know his intentions are ultimately good." Cody had a pinched look, like it was hard for him to say the words. "You could be happy with me," he urged. "We could have a good life together."

Was he for real?

"I want to first make sure Obsidian's okay." His chest movements were shallow and he looked pale.

"The beast is strong. He will be fine," Cody countered with a sneer.

"We don't know that for sure. I will nurse the dragon back to health. Once he is well again, you will have my answer... not that I'll have much of a choice." She shook her head.

"No. I don't want you anywhere near it. What will the pack say?"

"No one needs to know. You can have your goons stand guard outside. If the dragon dies without a proper trial, it could spell war with the dragons."

"He won't die," Cody snorted.

"You don't know that for sure. You can tell everyone I'm

distraught. Tell them that just knowing the dragon is on our territory has frightened me to my core after what happened. I'm at home and don't want to see anyone."

She could see Cody was thinking about it.

"That way, you kill two birds with one stone. I don't like his color… or how hard it is for him to breathe." The wheezing seemed worse to her. Thing was, Demi *was* really worried about Obsidian. No one else from the village would go anywhere near him. They were afraid of him. "I need to help him. I don't want him to die."

He shook his head. "I don't know."

"Please."

"No one from the village is to know that you are in there with him. Thankfully we are quite far away so no one should pick up your scent." He was talking more to himself, his eyes lifted in thought.

"Okay. Understood." She nodded.

Cody smiled, reminding her of the Cody she had once known, which hurt since not much of that male remained. "This will work out, Brie. You…"

She clenched her jaw. They kept their eyes on one another for a few seconds. He wasn't even going to apologize this time. "Open the cage."

He seemed to hesitate. To be rethinking the whole thing.

"No one else will agree to go in there with him. It has to be me. I refuse to give an answer until I know for sure he's going to make it. You know my answer if he dies."

Cody kept his eyes on hers for a few more seconds. "Fine," he sighed. "I will open it for you. I'll have Brutus fetch you the supplies you will need. My males will stand guard. No one will be allowed near this area and this stays between us."

"Yes, and thank you." The words tasted bitter on her tongue.

"Don't do anything stupid, Demi," he emphasized her name. Like saying it would erase all the times he'd called her by her dead sister's name. It wouldn't. He pursed his lips for a second. "It would kill your father to have to watch you being put to death as well. Not to mention what it would do to your mother."

"Don't bring my family into this." She inhaled deeply, trying to calm herself down. "I would never break our vows." She kept her voice neutral. "So you can stop with the threats already."

He raised his brows, like he didn't believe her. "I would have to release you from your vows before…"

"I know how it works." She sounded exasperated, which was good since she felt the emotion to her core. "I would never break my vows, okay? I'm not that kind of person and neither is Obsidian." Even though those promises were made under duress, she would honor them.

"Just so you know, it's never going to happen. I'm never releasing you from your vows." He looked so sincere. "I would rather die first. So do the right thing. Save the dragon. Save your people."

Do the right thing? Cody wouldn't know the right thing if it jumped out and bit him.

"Twenty-four hours, Brie."

"For the last fucking time!" she screamed. "My name is Demi. Demi!"

"It doesn't matter." He shook his head. His eyes vacant. "I want you in my bed… our bed, so that we can finish this once and for all."

Horror.

Revulsion.

Fear.

Hate.

Loads of the stuff. Truckloads!

Cody unlocked the cage and she went inside. The door closed and the key turned. Yet, right then, she felt freer than she had in days.

CHAPTER 17

H e realized two things and both at once. Firstly, he was in serious pain. Secondly, there was something warm curled up next to him. Sweet, musky, good. The sweetness reminding him of sunshine and cookies. Things he loved. He groaned when he realized what the scent was.

Female.

His female.

No, not his. Fuck! "Demi," he ground out, the pain in his chest flaring and not only because he had been shot several times.

"Oh god! Stay still." She sat up, leaning over him. "Don't move or you'll start to bleed again." Her eyes were filled with concern. "Your wounds were made by silver-tipped arrows, so it'll take a bit longer for the damage to heal."

"I figured," he growled. It hurt to talk. "It was him," he clenched his teeth, "yellow-bellied fucker."

"Shhhhh. I know," Demi urged. "Don't say anymore." She put a hand on his chest. Not on the wounds, but close. He felt instantly soothed. Her dark eyes softened, and her lip trembled.

It was hard work, but he managed to lift a hand. To stroke her cheek. His hand fell back moments later. He felt weak. Like a day-old lamb.

"It's all my fault," she whispered. "You shouldn't have come back."

"*His*… fault," he gasped. "Protect… you… had… to." Why was she in there? Why had the bear allowed it? She had to have bargained to be there. What though? "Shouldn't be here," he managed. Whatever it was, it was too much.

"Here." She brought a bottle of water to his lips. "Drink."

He did as she said, feeling slightly better. The action also made him feel more tired.

"A little more," she urged, bringing the bottle to his lips a second time. Obsidian drank. His limbs feeling more and more heavy. He fought to stay awake, wanting to know more. Wanting to…

Seconds, minutes, hours. Obsidian wasn't sure how much time had passed, only that he felt somewhat better when he woke up. It was easier to breathe and much of the burning pain had subsided to something a lot more bearable. He was still weak though.

Demi held the water bottle to his lips when he stirred. "Drink. You need to get strong again."

This time, he was able to drink deeply. "Thank you." He wiped his mouth, his voice was thick and grating.

She inspected his chest. "The wounds are healing well. Would you like something to eat?"

Obsidian shook his head. "Not right now." The thought of food made him feel nauseous. "You shouldn't be in here."

Her face clouded. "Of course, I should. I still can't believe he shot you like that."

Obsidian managed a smile, although it probably looked more like a grimace. "At least he got me in the chest, I would've expected a coward like him to go for the back... that's something at least."

She nodded once, looking worried. "He's an ass! I don't want to talk about him. How are you feeling?"

"I'm going to be okay, considering." He took her hand in his. "Thank you for being here and for helping me, but you should probably go. I didn't mean to cause any more trouble for you. I needed to be sure he wasn't... hurting you. I wouldn't put it past him. That male is unstable."

"You see it too?" Her eyes brightened.

"Yes," he nodded, "I do. It's why I haven't been able to stay away. One of the reasons at any rate."

She looked relieved. "No one else does. They all think I'm being difficult. Even my father. He wouldn't listen when I tried to talk to him earlier. He's known Cody his whole life. I guess he struggles to believe he could be like this."

"He should have listened." He frowned "You shouldn't be here though. I can't believe Cody would lock you in here. I can only think that you must have made some sort of deal with him. Which worries me. You're making things more difficult for yourself."

"I'm the only person in our village willing to be in here with you. You needed help. Cody can't have you dying on him. He'd be in big shit with your people if anything happened... wouldn't he?" She looked worried.

"I was trespassing, so technically, he could have killed me and gotten away with it. My brother warned me not to come but I didn't listen."

Demi looked down. She let go of his hand, picking at the quick of her nail.

"What is it?"

"That's what I was afraid of." She sighed. "I wish this hadn't happened but you're going to be fine." She brightened up, her eyes locking with his. "You'll be better in a day or so and they'll let you go."

His eyes narrowed. "I doubt that. There must be some sort of punishment they plan on meting out."

"I spoke with Cody. He will let you go once you're healed. You'll probably have to swear never to come back onto our territory again." Her eyes were dark and hazed over for a moment and then she smiled. "It'll be okay. He'll let you out of here. You'll have to swear though and stick to it."

It was just as he had imagined. Demi had made a deal with the devil. "That's not going to happen."

She frowned. "You have to do what they say, Obsidian. We enjoyed an amazing night together. We are highly compatible and…" He watched her throat work. "I happen to like you very much, but this thing between us has to end. You can't check in on me, you can't protect me. You can't ever come back again."

"You just asked me if Cody was unstable and I agreed, yet you expect me to leave you with him… just like that?"

"Yes." She nodded. "He is my mate. I hate the idea. I wish it could be different, but it isn't. I need to face facts and—"

"I thought you were fighting the mating."

"Is that why you keep coming back?"

The million-dollar question. He shifted, grimacing at the pain that flared in his chest. "My main reason for coming back was to ensure your safety. No one else in your pack has been willing to do that. I felt compelled. I couldn't just leave you to your fate. And yes," he pushed a breath out through his nose, "I did… and still do hold hope that you won't be forced to complete your mating with that fucker, that we— "

"Stop right there." She looked stricken. "Don't say anything more. You're wasting your breath. My mating isn't going away. In order for that to happen, Cody would have to release me from my vows, which he won't do. He already made that clear."

"I don't understand why he would want to force you into this. You will never be happy. I've never outright said this to you but don't do it, Demi." He shook his head. "Don't let them bully you. Let's escape… together… we can—"

"Please stop there!" She sounded stricken.

Obsidian bit down on his tongue to keep from finishing what he wanted to say.

"It can't happen." She shook her head.

He swallowed down his disappointment. "I know."

"The ridiculous thing is that I'm sure Cody will come to regret it if we finish the mating. He'll realize that he can't use me to replace Brie. I firmly believe that's what he's trying to do."

Obsidian nodded. "So, you're not going to go through with it then?" He could see instantly that she did plan on doing just that. "You will never be happy." There was urgency in his voice. "Please. I'm not saying this because I want a shot at something with you… I would love it, but that's not the main reason. I have no ulterior motive other than wanting to see you happy. You'll never be happy with Cody."

"I have no choice."

"There is always a choice. Your family, your people, that

male," he growled, "they would all have you believe that there is no choice but there is. They—"

"Cody is going to have you executed if I don't go through with it."

"That fucking coward!" he snarled.

"Surely he can't do that though, can he?" He could see panic well in her. "He plans on skewing what happened that night... making it sound like you forced me. Like I'm so distraught over what happened that I don't remember it clearly. So distraught, I can't even go through with the consummation of our mating."

"I also trespassed... several times." *Fuck!*

"He's going to spin it so that it looks bad... really bad. He wouldn't get away with it though, would he? Your people would fight it, wouldn't they?"

Obsidian nodded. "They would try. I'm not sure what kind of good it would do. The trespassing alone, especially when I was implicitly banned from coming back here... that might already be enough."

"To kill you?" Her voice was shrill.

"I broke that prick's ribs. I rutted you. I trespassed. He might just pull it off." His gut churned. "I will accept my fate though." He gripped her hand firmly in his. "Don't do it! Don't finish the mating because of me."

"What?" she half-yelled. "You can't be serious? I'm not letting them do this. I won't let them hurt you anymore."

"It's my choice and I—"

"It's *my* life. You came to protect me, and now I must do the same for you. You'll be decapitated with a silver blade and I will still be forced to stay in the mating anyway. It will have been for nothing."

"Fight this!" he urged.

"I can't. It's tradition. It's how things—"

"It's bullshit!"

"I know that. Unfortunately, the elders and the leaders of the packs feel differently. I have fought this. I've tried to change their minds. I've begged. I've pleaded… I've done everything I can think of. None of it has helped. I refuse to stand by and watch them kill you, Obsidian. To watch them accuse you of things you didn't do. I care too much to let that happen."

His chest warmed. "You care?"

She rolled her eyes, a small smile toying with the edge of her mouth. "Of course I do. I wouldn't be in this cage if I didn't."

"Don't do it! Don't go through with it, unless you change your mind about him. Forget about me and—"

"That's not going to happen. You have done everything to protect me. I mean," her eyes moved to his chest, "look at you. This happened because you were trying to help me. It's my turn to help you. I couldn't live with myself if something happened to you. I *can* help you."

"But at what cost? No, you—"

"We're not going to argue," she insisted. "We have ten hours left."

"Ten hours?" He frowned.

"Before I have to go to… before I have to leave you."

"To go to him?"

She didn't say anything. Her eyes told him everything he needed to know. Obsidian had to hold back a roar.

"I don't want to waste that time arguing," Demi went on. "You keep referring to your brother, Mountain, I think you said his name is. Are you guys close?"

Obsidian wanted to argue further. He had to try to change her mind. Instead, he nodded. "Mountain is my twin brother."

She gasped. "You have a twin?"

He nodded. "Yes and to answer your question, yes, we are close. My brother is my best friend. I could not imagine losing him. I cannot comprehend how it must have been for you to lose your sister."

"Terrible." She looked down at her hands and then back up at him. "Are the two of you identical?"

Obsidian nodded. "Yes, although, not completely. There are subtle differences. The biggest though, are our personalities. I am a loner. I do not fit in at all. I have been told that I don't play nice."

"I would have to disagree." Demi smiled. It was sad, twisted his heart and his gut. "I think you're one of the nicest people I have ever met."

"Thank you, Demi." He smiled back. "Mountain is well liked. He is the highest-ranking of the non-royals."

"Oh yes, I forgot about that. You guys have kings and queens."

"Yes, the royals have golden markings, where we have silver."

"I prefer silver." She put her hand back on his chest for a moment. Her touch felt like heaven. "Your wounds are looking much better after your rest."

"I am beginning to feel… more myself."

"Tell me more about your royals. Who is your king?"

"His name is Granite. He is mated to a human female."

"I hear that, like the vampires, your species is taking many humans. Ours are too."

"Yes." Obsidian nodded.

"Where are…?"

"I don't want to talk about my king or human females. I want to know about you, Demi. I know we will never be together, but I will feel better having known you… even if it's just for a few more hours."

"Okay." She smiled shyly. "What do you want to know?"

"Your favorite food. We can start there."

"That's easy… ribs. It doesn't matter which form they're in. The only thing that changes is whether or not they're basted and grilled or raw."

"Your wolf likes basted ribs on the grill?"

She grinned ruefully. "Yeah."

He chuckled, clutching his chest and grimacing when his wounds pulled tight.

"Are you okay?" She leaned over him, her eyes filled with concern.

"All good!" he pushed out. "Now, tell me what you enjoy doing. Do you have any hobbies?"

"Baking. I love to bake. My favorite is making all kinds of cookies."

He sucked in a breath. "No! I love cookies… in fact, I happen to think you scent of them. The vanilla kind with real butter and sprinkles on top."

She smiled shyly at him. "Really? Cookies?"

He nodded. "Cookies are my favorite." Just like Demi… a firm favorite. There was this tugging inside him. "You definitely scent of them."

She broke eye contact. Breaking the moment. "Um… my baby brother also loves cookies. His name is Serge," she spoke quickly. "He's a real goofball. I think you guys would get along."

"I do too. Do you have any other siblings?" And boom, just like that, sadness was back and he could have damn well kicked himself for being the one to cause it. "Mountain is my only sibling," he quickly added. "He recently mated."

"Oh." Her eyes brightened. "Good for him."

"It's quite a funny story actually... how he and Page met."

Demi leaned down on her thighs, getting comfortable. "I can't wait to hear all about it."

"He was on the hunt."

She frowned. "Hunting for deer?"

Obsidian grinned. "Not deer, no – humans. He was hunting humans."

"Humans?" Her brows lifted in shock.

Obsidian chuckled. "Let me tell you about the hunt first and then we'll get to Mountain and his initial meeting with Page."

She nodded once, waiting for him to continue.

They must have talked for a good couple of hours. Both of them trying to avoid what was coming. The clock kept on ticking. Obsidian wished he could stop it. Wishing even harder that he could do something to stop where this was headed. He'd never felt more useless in all of his life and it had nothing to do with the holes in his chest. All of them felt like they were right through his heart.

CHAPTER 18

The talking woke her up. She wasn't sure when she had even dozed off. Sometime after Obsidian had fallen asleep.

"Listen to the female," someone urged. "She is right," he spoke under his breath.

Demi turned over onto her back.

"She's awake," the same person said.

She sat up, rubbing the sleep from her eyes, when she took in the male on the other side of the bars. "You must be Mountain." She couldn't believe how alike they were. Their bone structure, their eyes… everything. Mountain's hair was a touch shorter, a little more styled but otherwise, they were carbon copies.

"Hello," another male said, he was standing next to Mountain.

"Hi, I'm Demi." She waved a hand, feeling a little unsure when she saw the golden tattoo.

"I'm Shale," he smiled.

Obsidian growled softly, it sounded like a warning.

Demi looked down at him, noticing how he had pulled himself up into a semi-reclining position. "How are you feeling? Do you want some water?" She lifted the bottle.

"I can see why you are taken," Shale said.

"Stop that!" Mountain growled. "My lord," he quickly tacked on. "You're not helping things."

"The wolf is quite a pretty thing… doting too."

"Demi," Obsidian snarled. "Her name is Demi."

Shale nodded once. "No need to be testy. I see what you mean," the prince addressed Mountain. "Obsidian definitely has feelings for the female, despite them not knowing each other very long."

"We are just friends," Demi interjected. It wasn't entirely true, since friends weren't supposed to be attracted to friends.

Shale snorted. "Not a chance. No wonder your mate, the Alpha, is so pissed off at this whole situation."

Obsidian growled low. His whole chest vibrated. His teeth looked like they had sharpened slightly. "Demi was forced to mate that prick."

"I know the whole story," Shale said, sounding bored. "Mountain filled me in." He looked her way. "The fact of the matter is that you are mated."

"They haven't—"

He put up a hand. "I know it hasn't been consummated. I have a nose… last time I checked I wasn't an idiot."

Obsidian clenched his jaw. "I just got out of a meeting with the Alpha and what he had to say was damning."

"All lies," Obsidian snarled. Demi put her hand on his chest and he instantly calmed.

"Not all of them." Shale shrugged. "You did rut his

girlfriend."

"Girlfriend my ass!" Obsidian muttered.

"That's what promised means. The female... Demi was his girlfriend at the time."

"I hadn't agreed to anything, so that's not technically true."

"The male thinks she was his girlfriend at the time, and you rutted her. Several times if I'm not mistaken. You trespassed and had your wicked way with her. Unfortunately, you picked the wrong female. Then you proceeded to beat up the Alpha when he called you out on it."

"That's not how it happened," Obsidian snarled.

Shale ignored the outburst. "You trespassed several times more, threatening not just to beat but to kill the Alpha."

Obsidian rose up to a sitting position. His muscles bulged. "The fucker deserved it!" he shouted.

"I know he did." Shale nodded once. "Again, Mountain filled me in, but it looks bad. It looks seriously fucking bad. To make matters worse, he's hinting that the rutting wasn't completely consensual. He says you are having a hard time being with him... sexually because you can't get that night out of your mind. Now I know that it's probably really because you want more of that," Shale spoke to her, pointing at Obsidian, "and none of that." He pointed behind him, to where the door was located. Hinting at Cody.

Demi felt her cheeks heat.

"He's spinning it differently," Shale said.

"I know," Demi replied.

Shale suddenly looked serious, turning to Obsidian. "That male will take your head." He paused, letting the words sink in. "He has called a meeting in an hour."

Her twenty-four hours would be up then.

"He is going to decide on your fate," Shale said. "You need to take Demi up on her offer."

"That's bullshit and—"

"He's right," Demi said. "I've been trying to tell Obsidian that. We don't have a choice here."

"There is always a choice." Obsidian's eyes blazed.

"If the choice is life or death," Mountain growled. "Your life or your death, brother. That's what we are talking about here, and if that is the choice, you need to listen to Demi."

"That's fucked up!" Obsidian whispered. He turned his gaze to her. "We're talking about a lifetime here. You would have to spend it with him."

"We are talking about your *life,* Obsidian," she urged, trying to get through to him.

"He has enough on you to make this stick." Mountain clenched a fist, frowning heavily. "He has witnesses to back him up. The blood and your seed in that clearing. His bruising after you attacked him. Your threats to him will be his word against yours but I know what others will think."

"It is settled," Demi said. "I am going to accept Cody. Accept our future together, even if it's not what I want. It is enough that everyone knows it. Deep down… they know."

"It shouldn't be enough and you shouldn't have to do this." Obsidian's beautiful chestnut eyes bore into hers.

"It's how it has to be." She felt like gasping out a sob when he finally nodded.

"Thank scale!" Mountain growled, sounding relieved. "I didn't think you would back down."

"Too stubborn for your own good," Shale remarked. "Do not worry female, we will take good care of Obsidian."

"Who is going to take care of Demi?" His eyes were still on her. They were filled with concern.

Her heart hurt with every beat. "I can take care of myself." She pulled her shoulders back.

"You shouldn't have to," he said, under his breath. Then Obsidian turned to the others. "You can go now, please. Give us some space."

He didn't look back at her until the door clicked shut. "I'm sorry," he said. Like it was his fault. Demi had never met anyone more powerful and yet so incredibly sweet.

"I don't think we would be breaking any rules if we hugged now."

Obsidian's lips twitched. "No," his voice was a deep rasp. "I don't think we would." He put his arms around her.

It felt so good. Like no one else existed in the world but them. "Don't let me go just yet."

"I will never let you go," Obsidian murmured. "Never."

If only it was true. If only. She hugged him tighter.

Obsidian wore a pair of cotton pants that his brother must have brought for him. The wounds on his chest were now puckered pink scars. Except for the one closest to his heart – that was scabbed over. Not as healed as the others. She couldn't take her eyes off of it. Couldn't take her eyes off of him. He was standing tall, jaw tight, muscles taut. He looked the picture of health, but she knew the silver was still taking its toll on him. There was a light sheen of sweat on his brow and his color was a little on the pale side. The sooner this was over with the better.

Everyone from their village was in attendance. She couldn't help but notice how the bears were to one side and the wolves to the other. A clear division. They were in the square. Everyone wanted to see the dragons. They wanted to see the male who had caused all the trouble. Obsidian was shackled. Hands secured behind his back like a criminal. Demi swallowed thickly. She'd protested against the silver restraints, but her requests had fallen on deaf ears. Nothing new there!

She smoothed a hand over her dress, standing proud. Demi needed to remain calm. She wasn't going to show any emotion. How angry she was. How hurt. How scared. None of that mattered. Only Obsidian mattered. His life mattered. If she showed any of the things she was feeling, he wouldn't go through with this. She knew he would end up sacrificing himself and she could not allow that to happen.

Cody cleared his throat. He was standing next to her. "Thank you all for coming," he addressed the crowd. "I would especially like to thank the Earth Prince, Shale, for making the trip. I only wish it could have been under better circumstances. One of your earth dragons has been trespassing on our territory. That male," he pointed, "Obsidian, came onto our lands and abducted one of our females."

Obsidian clenched his teeth, his eyes narrowed. Demi had to bite her tongue.

Say nothing – Cody had warned.

"The dragon took my female," Cody growled, taking her hand. "Took her, and hurt her…"

Gasps and cries came from the crowd. Mountain growled low. Shale gripped the male by the forearm and shook his head.

"I want to spare Demi any further pain and suffering," Cody shouted above the din, "so, we won't talk about that night." He put his arm around her shoulders, pulling her towards him.

How convenient. For him. If they didn't talk about it, the truth – namely, that nothing bad had happened – wouldn't be able to come out.

'Agree to everything I say without question,' Cody had made her promise.

"The dragon, Obsidian, blindsided me when I questioned him on his actions. He broke three of my ribs. The male wouldn't leave my female alone after that. Even after Demi and I mated. I expressly forbade him from returning to our territory. I said that I wouldn't take things further if he stayed clear of Demi and of Vale Creek, but he wouldn't listen." Cody pointed at Obsidian, who snarled.

Shit!

Don't. She shook her head once. Obsidian only made things look worse by retaliating.

"I was forced to take things into my own hands. I was fearful of the safety of my female." He closed his arm a little tighter around her. It felt like a threat rather than a comfort. "That's why I shot the dragon. I couldn't have him coming here, scaring my female, putting all of our lives at risk."

Shale had his arms folded. He was staring daggers at Obsidian. Mountain's face was red. Both his fists were clenched.

Obsidian, surprisingly, looked relatively calm.

Cody pulled in a deep breath. He looked like he was wrestling with something. All a pretense, of course. One big lie to add on top of all the other lies. She burst inside. Wanting to say something, needing so badly to set the record straight. "I discussed all of the ins and outs of this awful situation with the Earth Prince. You see, we have a relationship with the dragons. None of the packs wish to put strain on that relationship. I am within my rights to call a trial… to ask for the dragon's head but I have decided against this course of action."

There was more gasping, more talk amongst the pack.

"I have come to a decision. Obsidian will return home with his brother and the Prince. He will never come back to our territory. He will never bother my female again. The dragons will mete out the necessary punishments." He looked in Shale's direction and the Prince nodded. "Do you agree to the terms, Obsidian?"

"No!" Obsidian spat out the word, eyes narrowed on Cody.

A collective gasp went through the crowd. She felt Cody tense.

Her own mouth fell open. Why didn't he listen?

"I insist on being put to death," Obsidian said. "I forced myself on the female. I broke several of your ribs. I keep coming back and guess what… I won't stop coming back onto your territory. I won't stop harassing you, so you may as well take my head."

"No," Cody said, sounding confused. "You can go." He looked towards Shale and Mountain. "Take the male and keep him off our lands."

"They won't be able to do that." Obsidian shook his head. "Take my head!" he snarled. "That way you won't have any more hold over Demi, you sick fuck!"

"Stop!" Mountain bellowed. "Don't do this, Obsidian!"

Cody opened and closed his mouth. A look of horror on his face.

"What?" Obsidian, pulled at the shackles, which clanged.

"You don't know what to do now that you can't use me to manipulate Demi anymore? She doesn't want to be with you, and you won't use me to make her do what you want. Not happening. I would rather die." Obsidian sounded calm and fully in control.

"You heard the male," Cody snarled. "You heard his confession."

"No!" Demi yelled, pulling away from Cody. "Stop this! It's not true. None of it is. Obsidian has done nothing wrong. He didn't hurt me I—"

"My poor female isn't thinking straight," Cody said. "After her ordeal—"

"I'm perfectly fine!" she yelled.

"She is confused after all she suffered." Cody looked distraught, putting on an act even she was inclined to believe. "You heard the dragon. He forced himself on her—"

"Stop!" It was a voice she never expected to hear. Her father walked up to where Cody was standing. "This has gone far enough, and it needs to stop. Let the dragon go."

"How can you say that, Sampson? This is your daughter we're talking about. There is the male who hurt her." Cody pointed at Obsidian.

"I struggled to believe Demi when she told me you had changed. I thought she was exaggerating because she didn't agree with the mating. I kept holding on to my belief that our traditions needed to be upheld. That this mating needed to happen."

"It did! It does! Our traditions are all we have. There has been increased fighting between our two species. It wouldn't have happened if we had been properly mated," Cody countered. "Our traditions *do* need to be upheld, Sampson.

This male needs to be dealt with for—"

"All that male is guilty of is trying to protect my daughter. If Demi says he did nothing wrong, then I know he did nothing wrong. Come on, Cody! You are about to end a male's life to get what you want. That's not okay." He shook his head. "Maybe the power of being Alpha has gotten to your head. Or, it might be the love you have for my daughter that's making you behave irrationally. I'm not sure what's going on with you, but I do know this needs to end."

"I am the Alpha of this pack. Demi is my mate. Mine!" he snarled. "That male hurt her… by his own admission."

"He did nothing wrong," her father said. "He only said all that to protect Demi. To get her out of a bad situation. *You* are that bad situation, son. Do you even realize that?"

Cody barked out a laugh. "I am Demi's mate. That is crazy talk." He took her hand, gripping her hard.

Obsidian snarled, yanking against his shackles. The males on either side of him fought hard to hold him back.

"See. Look at that beast." Cody pointed. "It is feral."

"Do not talk about my brother like that," Mountain rasped. "Your lies are—"

Shale was holding him back. "Let this play out," the Earth Prince said, saying it more than once, until Mountain relaxed.

"He hurt your daughter," Cody spat. "Won't leave us alone. He keeps harassing her, she's told him to leave her be, but he won't listen."

"Obsidian didn't hurt me!" Demi yelled. She cried out when Cody squeezed her hand.

Obsidian snarled louder.

"My female is confused. That's all," Cody said. "Confused, right, sweetheart?" He glanced her way. Not waiting for her to answer. "I am the Alpha and my decision is final. That creature raped and hurt Demi. It attacked me. The male has trespassed three times on Vale Creek soil and keeps harassing Demi. I want it beheaded today."

"No!" she shouted, ripping away from his hold. "I am not confused. For the last time, Obsidian didn't hurt me."

"That isn't going to happen," her father said.

"My decision is final," Cody spat.

"There are six of us on the Council. I would need three more votes to counter this decision."

"Three votes you won't get." Cody narrowed his eyes.

Shit! Cody was right. Three members of the Council were wolves and three were bears. Her father would have a hard time getting the bears on his side. Especially with the packs so divided at the moment.

"Who will stand with me?" her father asked. "The only thing this dragon is guilty of is of loving my daughter. Of trying to protect her from Cody."

"That's absurd!" Cody spat. "I love my female with all my heart."

"The awful reality is that I do believe you, son, but you're taking this too far. This needs to stop. I vote to let the dragon go. To allow the dragons to leave safely, to return to their own lands. Who will stand with me?"

Within seconds, two of the Council members put up their hands. Both wolves.

"Thank you," her father said. "What of you, Thomas?" He looked at the male in question. Thomas frowned. After half a minute, he finally shook his head. "I'm sorry," he muttered.

"Mac? Will you do the right thing?" her father asked,

looking at the male in question.

Cody growled low, his lip curling away from his teeth.

The bear elder looked like he was deep in thought. It didn't take long for him to say, "Cody is our Alpha. The decision lies with him," Mac finally conceded. "I can't…" He shook his head, looking unhappy but sticking with his decision.

There was only one Council member left. Laird, Cody's father.

"There it is then." Cody grinned. "I am sorry to have to say," he bit back a smile, although his eyes still danced with malice, "but that leaves me with no choice but to—"

"I still have a vote," Laird interjected.

"What?" Cody frowned. "Surely you would side with the bears? With me? I am your son. I have Demi's best interest at heart. You have my word on that."

"Bears, wolves… we are all one pack. I refuse to take sides," Laird said. "I have known Demi for many years. She is a level-headed female who—"

"Who suffered an ordeal," Cody insisted.

"The dragon can go," Laird said. "I agree with Sampson. I'm sorry I didn't listen to you, old friend." Laird nodded in Sampson's direction. "I'm listening now. You can go, dragon," Laird addressed Obsidian.

"What of Demi?" Obsidian asked. "She is not safe with that male."

"Bullshit!" Cody snarled. "I love my female. You want to steal her from me, you bastard!" he spat. "For that and for that alone, you deserve to die."

Finally, a hint at the truth.

"Stop, son!" Laird looked tired. "I think Demi should go

home to visit with her parents until we get this—"

Cody roared. He lunged for Demi, pulling her into his arms. "No one is taking her from me."

"What is going on with you?" Laird asked. "I'm worried. I've noticed some changes in you, but I never imagined it was this bad."

"I am worried too," her father agreed, frowning. "Let Demi go, please, Cody. Let's discuss—"

"I will complete the mating and we *will* be together." Cody held her against him, holding too tight. "She is mine. I need her. I—" He squeezed her even tighter.

Obsidian roared. He broke free from one of his captors. The shackles rattled.

"Let me go!" Demi shouted. "Let me…" She elbowed Cody who wheezed as her arm connected with his diaphragm. His hold faltered and she broke free.

Demi took one stride away from him before he yanked her back. She was done with being afraid. *Done!* She turned, closed the distance between them and kneed him in the balls. Cody groaned as he crumpled to the ground. He reached out to her. "Brie," he groaned. "Please… don't leave me. You can't go. Not again."

Demi shook her head. "She's gone, Cody. My sister is gone."

"No." Tears trickled down his cheeks. "Don't say that! Don't you say that. Come back, Brie." He held his arms open. "We can be together again. Everything will be fine if you just…"

"Come, son." Laird helped Cody to his feet. "Let's go home."

"No," Cody raged. "No!" He swung a fist at his father.

Within seconds, several males had Cody in a hold. "Leave me!" Cody yelled. "Brie!" His eyes were wild, darting around the crowd until they landed on her. "Come back!" he shouted. "Please!"

It was only when a drop of wet landed on her chest that she realized she was crying. It was worse than she ever suspected. Cody was a complete mess. He was suffering a mental breakdown.

She was still technically mated to him too, which meant that her life was one big mess as well.

CHAPTER 19

Later that day...

O bsidian knocked on the door. It wasn't long and Demi's father answered. "Hello, sir." He bowed his head when he spoke as a sign of submission and respect. He half expected the male to turn him away.

Instead, he was greeted with a smile. "I'm Demi's father, Sampson." He held out his hand.

For a few seconds, he was too gobsmacked to do anything but stand there. "Um... yes... I'm... I'm Obsidian," he finally answered, clasping the male's wrist.

"Thank you." The male's eyes became watery. "For being there for Demi. You knew there was something going on. You... I mean," he shook his head in thought, "we knew she had taken her sister's death hard and we knew she was opposed to the mating, but we didn't realize... I just didn't realize what was really going on with Cody. You knew though, you just knew." He shrugged.

"I have learned over the years to look beyond words. I

always tended to speak less and observe more. It is just the way I am wired. Others haven't always understood me because of it. I always wished I could be more normal. Now I'm happy I am the way I am because I was able to help Demi. I could see she was in trouble. Your daughter is… she is wonderful." It didn't come even close to describing how amazing Demi was.

"Yes, she is." He nodded. "I have resumed the role as Alpha… at least for the time being. I just wanted to say that you are welcome on our soil… in our skies too, for that matter." Sampson smiled.

"Thank you, sir."

"Are you going to leave the poor male in the doorway for the whole evening?" a female called from inside.

"Oh, where are my manners?" Sampson stood to the side. "Won't you come in?" Obsidian did just that. "This is my mate, Delila," the older male continued.

Obsidian inclined his head. "It is good to meet you."

"Oh my." Delila smiled. She reminded him of Demi, only her hair was brown rather than black and there were a few lines around her eyes, which were just as dark and lovely. "I can see why my daughter is—"

"Obsidian," Demi interrupted. "You're here." She was smiling brightly.

"Yup." He wanted to smile, but his lips didn't work right then. "I thought I would check in. Make sure you're okay." He had to fight back a wince. What a stupid thing to say, of course she was okay, she was with her family. Away from Cody. "Also, to come and say goodbye as we are leaving soon." Demi had left with her parents after the whole incident earlier.

"Let's give these two some space," Delila said.

Sampson nodded.

Obsidian waited for them to leave.

"Would you like something to drink?" Demi folded and unfolded her arms, looking towards a door he assumed led to the kitchen.

"No… thanks." He shook his head.

"I…" they both said at once. Demi laughed, sounding nervous.

He smiled.

Demi swallowed thickly, he watched the column of her neck work. "I just wanted to say thank you… for everything."

Shit! For claw's sake… this sounded like goodbye. He hated that so much. Then again, she had said that she was fond of him. That she thought he was sweet… so… *Fuck!*

He nodded once. "No problem. Any time and I mean that… any time you're in a bind or…" *lonely,* "just any time you need… a friend." *Fuck!* Why had he said friend?

"Thanks." She toyed with a button on her sweater. "I really mean it. Thank you so much. I don't even know what to say or how to convey just how grateful I am. You told Cody to execute you, for goodness sake!" Her eyes turned stormy. "It did piss me off some when you did that. Especially after we agreed you—"

"I couldn't let you go through with it."

"Even if it meant dying? That's nuts, Obsidian. You don't even know me that well."

"I couldn't just stand by and watch you throw your own life away." He shrugged. "I would have done it for anyone." *Not true! Not at all!* He needed to shut the fuck up. He of all people. The male who didn't say something unless he had to. Unless he meant it. Unless completely pertinent. Yet here he was spewing shit. His mouth kept moving, more and more bullshit flooding out.

"Oh… okay then." Her smile widened. Like his false admission made her feel better. "So, you're heading back now?"

"Yeah, in a couple of minutes, but I couldn't leave without…"

"Saying goodbye."

He nodded once. *Telling you how I feel about you.* He had to tell her. Had to. Surely she knew though? "I just wanted to… I…" He took a deep breath. "I want to see you again, Demi."

There. It was out. Mostly. There was a ton more but that was a good start.

"Oh, yes… I mean, that would be nice."

Nice?

Fuck.

She must have seen the look on his face because she continued. "You know I'm still mated right? Nothing has changed. Not really."

"Surely they won't make that stick."

She shrugged. "I don't know anything yet. I took the vows. I made promises…" She rubbed a hand over her face.

"It was all under duress. They were just words at the end of the day. I don't believe so much in words." He cupped her jaw. "I believe in the feeling I get when I look into your eyes. When I touch you."

Her heartrate picked up and her breathing turned a touch ragged. Then she pulled away. "I believe in those things too. In fact, I told Cody much the same things. That they were only words, but in the eyes of my people they were binding. Technically, only Cody can release me and he… he isn't well." A look of concern crossed her face. "He isn't normally like this. He isn't being himself."

"Do you have feelings for him?" Jealousy, the big green monster reared its ugly head.

"No. Not like that. Thing is, I don't really know my feelings about anything. It's all just such a mess. I think I need some time to figure things out. To figure out what to do about my mating. About how I feel about you. These haven't been the best of circumstances and sometimes people feel things they normally wouldn't because of the situation they find themselves in. I like you a lot." She stared into his eyes. "I don't want to end up hurting you. Let me figure things out. Let me work through some stuff first."

"Okay."

"Give me your number. I'll call you when I'm ready."

"Oh shit!" He scrunched his eyes shut.

"What is it?"

"I don't have a phone. I'm kind of backward that way. I've never needed or wanted one."

"Email then?" She raised her brows.

He shook his head. Feeling like an idiot. "I guess I'm old school." He had a thought. "I know! I can give you my brother's number. Maybe you could message him?" He tried not to sound too eager. Too pushy. "When you are ready that is. I'll see about getting a phone in the meanwhile."

"Don't do that on my account. I can always send Mountain a message… for you." She shrugged.

"Sounds good." He gestured to the door. "He and Shale are waiting outside. I have no idea what his number is."

She nodded. "Let's head over there then."

Things were suddenly even more awkward between them. He wanted to roar in frustration. He followed behind her, trying not to notice how fantastic her ass looked in those jeans. Her long hair was glossy down her back. It smelled of berries and sunshine. He tried hard to ignore all of it. She wasn't ready. Not yet. Soon. Hopefully very soon.

Shale and Mountain were waiting a little distance from the house. They were talking about the slayers. Various precautions they were taking. Shale gave Mountain a bump with his shoulder, gesturing with his eyes to them as he saw them approach.

Mountain's eyes widened as he took them in. He smiled, looking uncomfortable.

"I need you to give Demi your number," Obsidian half barked at Mountain. He cleared his throat. "I don't have a phone or a computer, so she won't be able to get hold of me otherwise."

"No problem." His brother searched inside a leather bag he had brought along, fishing out his phone. He pushed a few buttons.

Demi did the same with her phone. Mountain told her his number. Things got a bit weird after that. Mountain looked down at his phone and then at Demi and then back down at his phone.

"Well," she said, licking her lips, "it was nice meeting you." She spoke to Shale and Mountain. "I'm truly sorry about all the trouble."

"How is the male? The bear Alpha?" Mountain asked, putting his phone away again.

"He is… in a bad way." Her voice hitched. "Sorry, it's just

I've known him for so long. No one – not even I – realized how bad he was. His family is organizing help for him. They may need to take him into town." She shrugged. "It will be a long road, I'm sure. At least now he is showing emotion about Brie… and what happened. Anyway, I don't want to keep you any longer. I'm sure you have lives to get back to."

Mountain nodded. "Yes, my female will be waiting for my return."

"Goodbye, Demi. Take care of yourself," Shale said, being uncharacteristically polite. Mountain also said goodbye, then ushered the prince a little away from them.

"You'll call then?" Obsidian winced. *Fuck!* He hadn't meant to say anything about that. "No pressure of course. You've been through enough. You had more than enough forceful behavior to last a lifetime. I won't do that to you. I won't come back unless you ask." He really prayed she would call.

"Thank you. That means a lot. I meant what I said, I like you a lot. I'm so grateful for everything. If it weren't for you…" Her eyes filled with tears. "You saved me."

"I would do it a thousand times over."

"Of course you would. You're such a sweetie."

"Not really," he tried. Hating the tone this conversation had taken.

"What do you mean?" She frowned.

"My nickname is Savage. I don't train a lot or have very much to do with the other males because I tend to hurt them by accident. Hence the nickname. I'm not sweet or kind or nice." His voice had turned gruff. "At least, that's what they would tell you."

She shrugged. "I would disagree because I think you are.

I don't care what the others say. Or what they call you. Being sweet and kind is a good thing. A compliment." She touched the side of his arm.

He pushed out a heavy breath. "Okay then."

"I mean it. I know you're a bad-ass as well. There's nothing wrong with being nice, you know?"

He nodded.

"I guess this is goodbye then," she said.

Why did it feel permanent? "I guess so." He opened his arms. "Can I have a hug?" Such a pussy thing to say but he wasn't sure what to do or how to react. He had no idea where he stood with this female.

She smiled. It made his chest hurt. "Of course." She put her head against his chest and hugged him hard. It was over too quickly for his liking.

"I'll be seeing you then, Obsidian." She gave him one last smile before she turned and walked away.

He watched her the entire time, hoping she might glance back at him, but it never happened.

"Bummer!" Shale said as he approached Obsidian. Mountain wasn't far behind.

Obsidian grunted. He didn't feel much like talking. Didn't feel much like anything.

"I wouldn't hold my breath for a call if I were you," Shale went on.

"You don't know that," Mountain objected. "Leave Obsidian alone."

Obsidian couldn't help but frown. "Why do you say that?" he asked, looking in Shale's direction. "She might call. We have a… *had* a connection. You wouldn't understand." He shook his head.

"Yeah, leave it be," Mountain said, widening his eyes at Shale. Like he was trying to convey something. Then he turned to Obsidian. "I will let you know the minute anything comes through."

Shale made this noise. He sounded skeptical. "I don't want him waiting around. That's all. Don't wait around," he directed at Obsidian. "I know females, and I know the wolf isn't going to call. She gave off all the wrong signals." Shale looked solemn and very serious. "I'm not trying to be a dick here. I can see how much the female means to you."

"What signals?" he finally asked, even though he could guess.

"The biggest clue was not giving her number." Shale raised his brows. "She gave the whole 'I'll call you' thing. Mountain was ready to take her number and she blew him off. That's never a good sign. Trust me! If a female is serious about staying in touch, she will always give her number."

Fuck! Shale was right. He never even thought of that.

"Then calling you a sweetie." Shale whistled. "Kiss of death, bro. She put you in the friend zone."

"You don't know any of this for sure," Mountain said. "Don't listen to Shale."

'Friend zone.' He'd never heard this term before. Unfortunately, he could guess what it meant.

"I've been with tons of females. I know females," Shale insisted. "Using words like sweet, kind and nice... nope, nope and nope. Sorry." Shale squeezed his shoulder. "I'm putting you down for the next Stag Run and I want you back in training. You showed integrity and restraint today. Mountain has always said that you would be an asset to our people, and I agree with him."

Obsidian should have felt happy at the compliment. He should feel ecstatic. His mind was still reeling though. He felt... hurt. He couldn't blame Demi. She had never asked for anything that happened to her. She hadn't promised him a thing, but... still... it hurt.

"Think about it," Shale said. "It'll take your mind off things."

Obsidian nodded. All he could think about was Demi. He hoped to god that Shale was wrong but this weight on his chest told him otherwise.

CHAPTER 20

Two months later…

Demi's step faltered. For a second, she thought about backtracking. Then turning around and running – as fast as her legs would take her. Fear, guilt, anger… so much anger. It all came flooding back. Maybe the emotions had still been there all along. Only, dormant? She wasn't sure. They were back now.

Then she saw his shoulders shake. She heard his anguished sob.

Demi pulled in a deep breath. He was a big male. To see him on his knees like this. A crumbled mess. It made all of the anger she'd been carrying float away. It made her realize something for the first time. Something else she'd been holding onto. It made her see things more clearly.

Demi took a step towards Cody. To where he kneeled on the ground next to Brie's grave. She'd been avoiding him. The fact that she'd managed it for four whole days, since he'd returned to their village, was a feat. He made another sobbing noise. It tugged at her.

Would he want her to see him vulnerable like this? She didn't think so, but she needed to see it. Needed to see him like this. Grieving. It helped her to move forward. Chances were good, it would help both of them move forward. Demi walked over. She kneeled down next to him.

Cody started. He hadn't even heard her approach. He wiped his face and sniffed, tamping down on his pain. Packing it away.

Demi placed the wild flowers next to the headstone. "I'm glad you're back," she said simply.

"How could you be?" His voice still held the grief she'd seen moments ago. His eyes were still watery and bloodshot. "After everything I put you through."

"*You* weren't *you* though."

"I'm still a little lost." His eyes moved upwards. "Very lost."

"Lost, but you're *you* again. Brie's Cody."

He nodded. "I'm sorry. You were right about everything." He wiped his face. "I was trying so hard to replace Brie. I didn't want to believe she was gone. I refused to accept it. To acknowledge it. Psychologists at the hospital I stayed at said that it was because of my guilt over her death. I was riddled with it. I still am. I refused to accept that she was gone. I was unable to work through the denial stage of the grieving process as a result." He sniffed again. "I was willing to do anything to hold up the lie I was telling myself. I was in full denial over her death, to the point where I pretended you were her. I convinced myself that if we just mated, everything would be okay. That I would feel better. That you would be happy. I was wrong." He bowed his head, trying to gather his control again.

Demi touched her sister's gravestone and rose to her feet. She gave Cody a hand, helping him up to his feet.

"I realize now," Cody went on. "That it wouldn't have worked. You aren't Brie and the lie would never have held up. We don't love each other in that way." His face had a stricken look. "I'm working through the stages now. Trying to forgive myself, not only for the accident but for what happened with you as well."

"I need to apologize as well."

"What?" He frowned heavily. "No! Why? What could you…?"

"I blamed you for her death. I did!" A couple of tears leaked out. Demi swiped them away. "I never once told you that it wasn't your fault. I was angry with you. It wasn't just over the whole promised situation. It went deeper. I blamed you, Cody. I'm part of the reason you felt all that guilt. You tried to talk to me about it after the crash. You tried to explain and apologize but I shut you down." She shrugged.

He nodded once. "I wouldn't blame you if hated me. If you—"

"I don't! I didn't realize how angry I was… at you… for her death. I didn't realize until just now that I blamed you for her death and in so doing was harming you. I think that's why I was having those dreams about the accident."

"I heard you… every night. Some nights were worse than others, but they were all bad. I know that much."

"I still am."

"No." He looked concerned. "You're still plagued by the nightmares?"

"Yes." She nodded. "I dream I'm there. I see her die every night. The worst part of it all is that I hear you laughing. That's how I wake up, with you laughing. I didn't realize why. Now I know. It was like you killed her on purpose. Like you were happy about it."

"I'm so damn sorry. I hate myself." He sounded angry. "I swear it was an accident. A stupid, senseless—"

"No, don't. Please. I *do* forgive you. Not that there's anything to forgive. The accident was just that… it was an accident."

"I took my eyes off the road." His voice was anguished.

"We all have at one time or another. No one is perfect. None of us. It was bad luck! The worst luck. I know you loved Brie."

"With all my heart." He hung his head. "I miss her." His voice hitched.

"I miss her too." Demi bit down on her lip to keep herself from crying.

They stood in silence for a few beats. "I heard that our mating was dissolved a week or two after I left but I wanted you to know that I don't hold you to any of those vows. I wish none of that had ever happened. I wish I could turn back the clock and—"

"It's fine. I forgive you for all of that as well. It's related. You were in a bad place. I think you still are."

"It feels to me like I only just lost her, you know?" He got this look on his face.

"I know. I can see it."

"Thank you." He gripped her hand. "For your forgiveness, for your understanding. I can't tell you how much it means."

Demi felt so much lighter. "I'm glad I saw you today. Glad that we talked." She took a step back and then another.

"Me too."

She began turning away.

"Hey," Cody said, making her turn back to face him. "Whatever happened with that dragon? Obsidian." He smiled.

She shrugged. "I said goodbye to him the day you left. I haven't seen him since."

Cody frowned. "I thought the two of you... that you had something going."

"I'm not sure what we had."

"That male was smitten." Cody's smile grew a little wider. "Completely taken with you. Pissed me the hell off." He turned serious. "I had hoped that the two of you had made a go of it. I would have liked to apologize to him as well, although, he might have broken both my legs if I tried."

"I doubt it." Demi smiled. "He's a big softie."

"Softie," Cody snorted. "Maybe where you were concerned. Nothing soft about the male." He turned wistful. "I'm sorry to hear things didn't work out. I think you would have made a good couple."

"I'm sure he's moved on. It's been a while since we last saw each other."

"I wouldn't be so sure. He risked life and limb for you."

She giggled. "He would have done that for anyone."

"No damned way."

"You don't think so?" she asked, her mind reeling.

"I know he wouldn't have. I don't think I've ever seen such a hard male turn into such a..." he shrugged. "Maybe softie is a good word to use. That only happens when a male has fallen hard. There is no way he has moved on. He is most likely still waiting. Still holding out hope."

CHAPTER 21

Four days later…

Obsidian flew as fast as his wings would take him. He circled the pinnacle and raced back to the rock formation he had just left. Claws outstretched, he made quick work of the perched boulders, pretending they were the enemy. *Slam, slam, slam!* The rocks crashed to the ground below and dust billowed. He roared, racing back to the balcony, pushing himself… hard. Until his muscles ached and sweat beaded.

Breathing heavily, he slowed his flapping, easing down to the balcony below. He saw Mountain leaning against the far wall. He was fiddling with his cellphone. Mountain looked up as Obsidian began to shift. He looked tense and was frowning.

"What's wrong?" Obsidian's voice was still thick and rasping.

"Um… there's been a sighting on our southern border, near the quarry," Mountain said.

"Oh. That's a problem. What is being reported?"

"It's something strange that's come up on our new radar equipment. Something on the ground… moving at a high speed. I'm not sure if it's just a glitch in the system or a real potential threat. I would handle it myself, but Page is about to come into heat." Mountain shifted from one leg to the other. He got a pinched look that quickly turned goofy. It was a look Obsidian knew well. One his brother often got when speaking about his female. Hell, even thinking about Page made Mountain go all sappy. It was sickening to watch. "I want to take her to my cave. The sooner the better. I came over to see who was available to head to the southern border right now, to take care of it." Mountain looked up to where the males were still sparring with one another.

"Training on my own gets boring fast," Obsidian announced. "I quit early," he added.

"I can't believe they *still* aren't picking you as a sparring partner." Mountain shook his head.

"They all have good memories. They all still call me by that nickname." His voice turned gruff. "Will I ever be known as anything other than Savage? No one will give me a chance to prove that I'm not that male anymore. I have evolved."

Mountain shrugged. "You have broken bones and removed limbs, so I guess they all have a point. Keep going the way you are and I'm sure one of them will come around. It only takes one."

"You are right." Obsidian looked back up at the males. "They will be at least another twenty minutes. Why don't you give me those coordinates and go back to your female. I can't believe you're actually going to try for a whelp."

"You'll be an uncle." Mountain tapped him on the back, smiling broadly.

Obsidian grunted and gave a nod. At moments like this, he thought back about Demi. About everything that could have been. Then he felt stupid. It had been a few days of his life. He had probably only imagined the chemistry between them. The potential.

"Did you get that?" Mountain asked.

"Get what?"

"The coordinates," Mountain chuckled. "Pay attention this time."

"I'm ready." Obsidian gave his head a shake, needing to dispel wayward thoughts. "Come again."

He memorized the coordinates this time, even though Mountain insisted on giving them a third time to be sure. "The… bogey is headed in a northwesterly direction."

"Got it."

"If you spot something, don't engage unless you're sure you can handle it. Otherwise, call for backup. You have my number."

"Why would I call you?" Obsidian asked, frowning. "You're headed to your cave. I'll call for backup if need be."

"Be careful out there." Mountain looked concerned.

"I've got this," Obsidian said, already shifting back into his dragon form. He headed for the southern border and the coordinates Mountain had given him. He slowed down as he reached the approximate position. Obsidian kept his eyes on the ground. Why would the target be on the ground? It was much easier to fly through the dragon territory. It suddenly didn't make any sense.

He kept moving in the direction given. This was probably

a mistake. Their new equipment must be malfunctioning or—

Wait.

What was that?

A flash of black. *What? Hold up!* He knew what that was. It had to be… *No!* He must be mistaken. He headed in. Moving closer and closer. Careful at the same time, in case this was a trap.

Fuck!

There… right there. Sleek black fur. Long limbs. His heart just about beat out of his chest when he caught the creature's scent.

Obsidian roared.

The creature looked up at him. Dark, gorgeous eyes locked with his for a moment before she picked up speed. Running even faster than before. His heart galloped in his chest. Adrenaline pumped.

Hunt.

Hunt.

Every instinct rose up in him. Obsidian roared again. He took his time, enjoying the chase. Toying with his quarry. He loved watching how her fur caught the sun. How her paws ripped at the earth. Beauty. Pure, raw beauty at its finest.

It was only when she ground to a halt that he realized how close he was. The wolf turned to face him. Her chest heaving from the exertion.

Obsidian landed in front of her. His heart pounded. Need coursed through him, his beast recognizing her.

Hunt.

Take.

She took a step towards him and then another before

shifting. He watched as the most beautiful female he had ever seen slowly emerged. Long limbs, flared hips. Her nipples were dark and plump. Her skin olive and soft looking. Her hair was a tangle down her back. Her cheeks were flushed from the exertion. She gave him the once over, her eyes moving in a languid fashion. A smile toyed with one side of her lush mouth. It made him growl low. His chest rumbling. Then she turned and ran. Obsidian snarled as he followed.

Catch.

Hunt.

He let her get out slightly ahead of him. Then slowly gained on her, slowly. Steady. Obsidian could have taken her down an age ago, but this was far too much fun. She finally stopped, her breathing ragged. She was so close he could touch her. Her musky scent enveloped him. His nostrils flared as he took it in.

Obsidian shifted. It was difficult. It hurt. Shifting with an erection was not an easy feat. He groaned as he made the final change. He didn't touch Demi though. Not so much as a finger, which was difficult given how amazing she looked. Her back was long and sleek like her legs. Her ass was plump and rounded. He just stood there waiting. It didn't matter that his dragon was screaming for him to take her. To rut her.

"I take it there is no bogey at the southern border," he rasped. "There is no glitch on our radar, is there?"

Demi turned, a smile toyed with the edges of her lips and her beautiful eyes danced.

"You are the reason Mountain warned me not to approach unless I could handle it… when I can handle most things quite easily."

She nodded. "He was worried about you. Apparently, you struggled after returning home. He said you used to ask him to check his phone five times a day. That you drove him," she lifted her eyes in thought, "bat shit crazy… I think was the term he used."

Obsidian smiled. "He shouldn't have told you all that."

"He also said that he didn't want you getting hurt." She licked her lips. "Especially after you were doing so much better. You haven't asked him to check his phone in a week or two." She shrugged.

"He has been worried about me."

"Mountain asked me several times if I was sure about you before coming out here." She pulled in a breath. "And I am. I'm so sure. I have feelings for you, Obsidian. Real feelings. I'm sorry it took me so long to figure it out. You need to know that it was never you I had doubts about."

"The bear?"

"Yes, but not in the way you think. My sister's death… Cody… what happened… my nightmares… all of it. I had to work through all of that to get to a place where I knew things were real. My feelings for you were real and not just something I dreamed up to help get me through a difficult situation."

"I thought you had friend-zoned me."

She frowned. "Where did you get that idea?"

"I thought you only saw me as a friend. Shale warned me that you wouldn't call. He said you used words like kind, sweet and fond to describe me. I hated that you used fond." Obsidian shook his head. "Shale said that meant you saw me as a friend and only a friend. He has a great deal of experience with females."

"I *am* fond of you. I *do* think you're sweet and kind. I always thought you looked beyond stupid words though, because if you did, you'd know that I find you seriously hot as well." Her eyes dipped down, landing on his cock, which was still hard. "Friends don't want to do dirty things to friends."

"You want to do dirty things to me?"

"So many dirty things, and now that I am single I can do all the dirty things I want, as often as I want." Her face fell. "That is, if you haven't moved on. I know I took a long time to sort my issues out, but I was hoping we…" She looked down at the ground for a moment before locking eyes with him. "I asked Mountain how you were… if you were still interested in me… us… Your brother wouldn't tell me anything. He wouldn't…"

"You asked about me?" Obsidian grinned. He knew it would look goofy, but he didn't care.

"Mountain and I have been messaging back and forth for a couple of days."

"Days?" Obsidian frowned.

"Like I said, he was being protective. He finally agreed to this meeting. Look, I don't blame him. Two months is a really long time to make someone wait. Although I see you as sweet and kind, I'm also attracted to you – very much so. I have feelings for you, Obsidian. They're still there. They weren't imagined or invented. My life is far less complicated now."

"And you're free?" He raised his brows.

She laughed. "Yes, I'm most definitely available and I'm here to take you up on your offer."

"You want to mate me?" Excitement surged through him.

She laughed again. "Easy there. Your offer of spending some time with you. A couple of days," she looked around them, "out here. Getting to know one another. The best part is that my family knows I'm here, so there will be no search and rescue teams sent out this time."

"They know you are here with me?"

She nodded. "Yes, they do. I guess we've all learned a thing or two. They've learned to let me make up my own mind. They also happen to like you – very much." She smiled. "I happen to like you very much too."

"Yes," he nodded his head once, not wanting to look too eager, "that sounds great. I would love to get to know you. There are a great many things I don't know. We only had those few hours to talk so... shall we go and sit over there?" He pointed to an outcrop of rocks. "They would make a good—"

"We could start with sex." Her voice was laced with need.

His eyes flew to hers, which were glinting with mischief. "Um..." His cock was as hard as volcanic rock. His balls were pulled so tight they hurt. He hadn't wanted to go there right off the bat. There was no need to ask him twice though. "Yeah... of course!"

Hunt.

Take.

Rut.

His dragon rose up in him. Obsidian growled as he picked her up. Now that she'd asked, need rode him hard. It invaded his whole being. "Fuck." His mind had wandered to the wet place between her thighs. He could scent her arousal.

"Yes, please." Her voice thick with desire. "Put me down

here," she instructed. "I need you inside me," she half growled the words.

"So sexy," he rasped as he put her down, turning her around to face a tree. "Put your hands on the trunk." He growled as she lifted her ass in clear invitation.

Obsidian practically salivated as the scent of her pussy invaded his senses. His snout, his tongue. He could almost taste her. Sweet and juicy like a ripe fruit.

She was panting. Her fingers clutching at the bark. He was desperate but he didn't want to hurt her.

Obsidian slid a hand around her belly and into her folds, quickly finding that bundle of nerves. He rubbed her clit a few times, dipping down into her channel to find the wet that pooled there. Then he was back at her clit, rubbing softly.

Demi mewled and rocked against his hand. She arched back against him and nudged him with her ass. The head of his cock was there, at her slit. He could feel her warmth, how slick she was.

Take.

Rut.

Claim.

Oh fuck. He was going to have to put a rein on his dragon. His beast had decided Demi was his. As in, for life. He nudged into her, snarling as his cock sank into her warmth.

"Yes! Oh… yes… more!" she yelled, rocking back against him.

He nudged in deeper and deeper still, making the most obscene snarling and growling noises with each thrust. If anyone was in listening distance, they would think he was killing Demi, who was shrieking with each plunge.

Obsidian bottomed out with a snarl, trying to ease off on her clit. He was a dragon for fuck's sakes. This needed to last longer than half a minute. He sucked in a couple of deep breaths, his finger tracing soft circles over her nub.

"Oh... oh god... oh... Obsidian..." It was a plea if he ever heard one.

"Hold on," he growled, the words barely recognizable. He clasped her hip with one hand, keeping the other firmly between her legs. Obsidian fucked his female. Putting everything he had into the action. All his frustrations. All his pent-up emotions. Everything. He put it all in there. The feelings he had for Demi. Feelings he didn't want to reveal just yet.

Her pussy spasmed hard around him. It was sudden and all at once. She gave a startled yelp. There was a moment of silence and then she screamed.

He put his hands on the trunk next to hers. Still thrusting into her... hard. Tight. Wet. Hot. So damned fucking tight. "Oh... shit... oh... Demi!" Then he was roaring as his own release took hold of him. His movements turned jerky. Her pussy spasmed so tightly around him he could barely move. His balls exploded. His eyes rolled back. His knees almost gave in from the sheer ecstasy of being inside this female again. His Demi.

He felt her slipping down, and gripped her around her waist, hoisting her back up against him. She was breathing heavily. She giggled, sounding out of it.

Obsidian could barely catch his breath.

"Holy crap." She giggled again. "No wonder they call you Savage."

He opened his eyes.

"You are savage where it counts." She giggled again. "Savage with your cock," she said between giggles.

That's when he noticed that he'd ripped a chunk out of the tree.

"Oops." He chuckled.

Demi turned around. Her arms draped around his neck. Her dark eyes were hazy. "You're savage in every way that counts. My sweet savage dragon."

Then he was lifting her up and slowly sinking back into her heat. "Let me show you just how savage I can be," he murmured into her ear.

CHAPTER 22

Ten months later...

"Today will be a sparring day," Stone explained.

Shouts of excitement went through the crowd of males.

Obsidian sighed. *Great!* The others might love one-on-one combat with one another. They loved the chance to test their skills, strength and agility. Sparring was fun. They didn't get days like this very often. It was a nice break in the monotony of patrolling the borders. Thing was, Obsidian was getting sick of trying to beat his best flying time. He didn't feel like lifting boulders or pretending to spar with inanimate objects.

"Pair up." Stone gave him a baleful look. "And head out."

The males paired up and as per usual, no one picked him. *Big shock!*

"Hey, Savage," Clay called.

His heart sped up. *Surely not? Surely...*

"You have a visitor," the male smirked, pointing behind

him.

Of course. How had he ever imagined that someone would pick him? Especially Clay of all males.

Obsidian turned, feeling instantly better as his eyes landed on Demi. So fucking gorgeous in that blue summer dress.

She grinned at him, holding out a paper bag. "You forgot your lunch. I specially baked and packed those cookies you love… the vanilla ones… the ones with sprinkles." She winked at him and his heart quite literally skipped a beat.

"You know me so well." He rushed over to her, enveloping her in his arms, taking in her amazing scent. "You didn't come because of the lunch. You can admit that, you know."

She shook her head. "It wasn't the lunch. You know me so well too." A smile played with the edges of her lush mouth.

"It was because you missed the hell out of me, admit it."

"Absolutely." She reached up and kissed him softly on the lips.

"What do you say we get out of here and…"

"Hey!" someone said behind him.

Obsidian turned. It was Clay. The male had a strange look on his face.

"What is it?" he barked, irritated that the male was interrupting his conversation. The idiot probably wanted to throw him some wiseass comment about not being picked… again.

"Would you like to pair up with me?" Clay asked.

Obsidian's frown deepened. "Pair up? Me?" He cocked his head. "Are you sure you're asking the right person?" He turned and looked behind him. There was no one there.

Clay grinned. "Yes, Obsidian, I'm sure."

What?

Had the male actually just called him by his given name? *Not a fuck!* "Are you sure?"

Clay rolled his eyes. "I'm very sure."

"You're not afraid?" Obsidian narrowed his eyes. *What was his game?*

"No!" Clay shook his head. "You've gone soft." He gave a one-shouldered shrug. "You're no longer that lonely, angry male I remember. In fact," he cracked his knuckles, "I think I might just be able to take you." The grin was back.

"Are you sure you want to goad me?" Obsidian narrowed his eyes on Clay, who laughed.

"I'm not worried." Clay shrugged. "Not anymore."

Cocky fuck! Obsidian grinned. "You warm up while I say goodbye to my mate and my whelps." He pulled her against him, putting a hand on her lightly rounded belly. "I look forward to kicking your ass."

"In your dreams, Obsidian." The male said his name like it was a taunt. "Good to see you." Clay waved at Demi, giving her a wink. Then he sprinted away.

Obsidian kept his eyes on Clay. Watching as the male shifted.

"You have a look in your eyes," Demi said. "One that doesn't bode well for Clay."

"I'm shocked!"

"It was only a matter of time before someone finally picked you. Mountain, Page and I have been telling you that for months."

"Not that?" Obsidian snorted.

"What then?"

"I don't like being called by my name." He felt bewildered. "For years I've hated that nickname…"

"Not when *I* call you Savage you don't." She looked at him from under her lashes and his dick took notice. It was not a good time for that!

He felt a goofy smile appear on his face anyway. "No," his voice was thick and husky, "not then."

She giggled. "I think I changed your mind about the name and now you like it."

"That must be it." He nodded.

She suddenly turned serious. "Don't hurt that male. I know you're tempted but don't do it." She wagged a finger at him in a playful manner.

"No, I think I'll hurt him some." Obsidian glanced at where Clay was flying above them.

"What?" Demi frowned.

"I won't break him, but I'll toy with him a bit… bring him down a level or two."

"No breaking anything though. No tearing off wings or…"

"That only happened once… the wing thing that is. It happened once and it was only one wing." Would anyone ever let him forget?

"Take it easy, that's all I'm saying." She circled her hands around his waist. "You've been waiting for a chance to spar for a very long time. Don't screw it up."

It wasn't just about sparring. It was about becoming a member of the team. A real member. "I won't." He nuzzled into her. "My voice of reason. I love you."

"I love you too." She kissed him. "My sweet savage dragon," she murmured as they pulled apart. Demi winked. "Now go and teach Clay a lesson." She patted him on the ass.

"Yes, my love."

"I'm going to watch. There might be a reward for you on the other side." She licked her lips. "One that would see me on my knees, using my mouth."

He swallowed thickly. "All I have to do is win?"

She choked out a laugh. "I know you'll win. Leave him in one piece. No broken bones, don't break anything and I promise to break you." She bobbed her brows.

He groaned. "That sounds good. I'll be back shortly."

"I'll be waiting." She put a hand to her belly and rubbed.

Obsidian took to the sky with a roar. Clay could goad him all he wanted. The only bait he was taking belonged to a certain wolf. The keeper of his heart.

CHAPTER 23

Shale walked into the bar. It was humming. Gorgeous females everywhere he looked. They frequented several establishments in this town. This one was by far his favorite. Excitement coursed through him. It had been six months, almost to the day, since he had last been there. Since he had last bedded a human female.

Several sets of eyes tracked him. This was his favorite part, picking the lucky female he would spend the night with. He would take his time about it too. No need to rush into anything.

"Look at *her*," Stone groaned, knocking a shoulder against him. "And the legs on the blonde," he continued.

The female in question winked at them, eyes on Shale. She wore a tiny dress and did, indeed have fantastic legs.

"You lucky fuck!" Stone grumbled. "You always get to pull the best females."

"Of course I do." He snorted. "I'm a prince."

"Yeah, but they don't know that," the male chuckled.

Shale shrugged. "They can sense it. Besides, I'm way

better looking than any of you assholes. Not to mention I'm better in the sack."

"Yeah, but again, she wouldn't know that."

"These females talk, and word gets around."

Ore arrived, fresh from the bar;, he handed them a couple of beer bottles. Shale and Stone said their thanks, chinking bottle necks with each other and with Ore. Shale drank deeply, watching as the others did the same.

Stone wiped his mouth with the back of a hand. "I guess it helps that you can have your pick of dragon females as well. It benefits being an unmated royal. Some of us have to wait long periods between ruts. We get... rusty."

Shale laughed. "Rusty and horny. Not really a great combination when it comes to rutting."

The male narrowed his eyes. "It's not so bad as that..." Then he stood a little taller, his attention back at the bar. "That female doesn't seem to like you much though."

Shale followed his line of vision. He recognized the female who was scowling at him but couldn't say when he had seen her before. He doubted she was one of the females he had bedded over the years, but he couldn't be completely sure.

Her jaw tightened and her eyes narrowed. She turned away, her eyes drifting over the rest of the patrons.

Stone chuckled. "One of your conquests?"

"I don't think so." Shale shook his head.

"I think you might be mistaken. She definitely recognizes you. All that anger doesn't come from nowhere. She probably wanted more and you cold-shouldered her."

Shale had a rule. He didn't rut a human more than once. They tended to become attached far too easily. "I doubt it but—"

Stone shoulder-bumped Shale again. "Hey look! She's coming over." Stone sounded animated.

It was the leggy blonde. Her gaze was still focused on Shale.

"Shit but she's gorgeous," Stone enthused.

"She's all yours," Shale remarked. The blonde was pretty but a little too eager for his tastes.

"She's here for you," Stone remarked.

"Trust me, she'll be all over you as soon as I leave."

"It doesn't get too much better than that," the male groaned.

Shale gave a one-shouldered shrug. "I'm pretty sure it does. Maybe even the next female to walk through those doors…" He gestured to the main entrance. Just then, the door opened and a female walked in.

"Oh fuck!" he growled when he saw who had entered. "Holy shit!" he added, realizing who the female at the bar was.

"Who's that?" Stone asked, sounding confused. "I'm not sure that female should even be in here." He frowned.

The female's eyes moved across the busy space, stopping when they locked with his. She clenched her jaw, looking as pissed as all hell.

"Hi there," the blonde remarked, stopping in front of them. Her timing could not have been worse.

Shale ignored her, keeping his gaze on the approaching female. Unable to move so much as an inch. Adrenaline flooded his system. That and the cold icy fingers of fear traced his spine.

"I'm Tina," the blonde said.

"Stone," his friend answered. "It's good to meet you. Can

I get you a drink?"

"You asshole!" the approaching female growled as she drew near. Her eyes were blazing. Her whole body radiated tension.

"Yes, thanks," the blonde sounded unsure.

Stone chuckled. "I hope this isn't what I think it is."

Fuck!

Oh hell!

Shale didn't say anything. Stone and the blonde walked away.

"You said I couldn't get pregnant," the female said, craning her neck so that she could keep her eyes locked with his. "You said it wouldn't happen. You said you were clean and that you were sterile." She waved an accusing finger. "Does this look like sterile to you?" She pointed at her distended belly. "I'm such an idiot," she muttered, more to herself.

"No." He shook his head. "It can't be." He shook it harder, frowning to the point where it felt like his face might crack. She hadn't been in heat though. Not even close.

"This is the part where you deny being the father. Well listen up, bucko… you are the only guy I've had sex with in a very long time. You and only you." She jabbed a finger into his chest again. "I picked you that night because I knew you wouldn't be interested in a relationship. You can relax – I'm not here to try to trap you or anything. I still don't want a relationship." She shook her head, her eyes welling with tears, but she quickly blinked them away. "I'm not ready to be a mother… I'm not…" More shaking. "I can't raise… can't possibly… I just can't do this!" She handed him a piece of paper. "Here."

As if on autopilot, he took it and lifted it. There was a

telephone number scrawled on the paper.

"My number," she said. "I'm due in three months. You have that long to decide if you want to raise this child." She touched her belly, the anger leaving her, sadness welling in her eyes. "Otherwise, it looks like I might have a great family lined up to adopt this baby. I can't keep it." She sniffed, her throat working. "I wish things were different but I... um... I just can't." She sniffed again.

Then she turned and walked away.

Shale had always been a rational male. He quickly thought things through. A couple of things were apparent. She was definitely pregnant, although he couldn't tell if the baby was a dragon or not. His or not. Not with so many warring scents. *His! Oh fuck!* He tamped down on the panic. He had taken her back to the hotel six months ago. The female at the bar was her friend. The same female had obviously tipped her off that he was there. *Fuck!* Shale couldn't remember either of their names.

More adrenaline spiked his system and he began to walk towards the female. This was a total cluster fuck of epic proportions. Three months. She'd told him he had three months. However, if she was pregnant by him, she was due *now*. Any day. Also, she was pregnant with twins. Not one but two. He was an Earth dragon after all. Lastly, they would not be human. She didn't know any of this.

Fuck!

The blood drained from his body and sweat beaded on his brow. Shale picked up the pace.

END

AUTHOR'S NOTE

Charlene Hartnady is a USA Today Bestselling author. She loves to write about all things paranormal including vampires, elves and shifters of all kinds. Charlene lives on an acre in the country with her husband and three sons. They have an array of pets including a couple of horses.

She is lucky enough to be able to write full time, so most days you can find her at her computer writing up a storm. Charlene believes that it is the small things that truly matter like that feeling you get when you start a new book, or when you look at a particularly beautiful sunset.

BOOKS BY THIS AUTHOR

The Chosen Series:

Book 1 ~ Chosen by the Vampire Kings
Book 2 ~ Stolen by the Alpha Wolf
Book 3 ~ Unlikely Mates
Book 4 ~ Awakened by the Vampire Prince
Book 5 ~ Mated to the Vampire Kings (Short Novel)
Book 6 ~ Wolf Whisperer (Novella)
Book 7 ~ Wanted by the Elven King

Shifter Night Series:

Book 1 ~ Untethered
Book 2 ~ Unbound
Book 3 ~ Unchained
Shifter Night Box Set Books 1 - 3

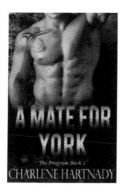

The Program Series (Vampire Novels)
Book 1 ~ A Mate for York
Book 2 ~ A Mate for Gideon
Book 3 ~ A Mate for Lazarus
Book 4 ~ A Mate for Griffin
Book 5 ~ A Mate for Lance
Book 6 ~ A Mate for Kai
Book 7 ~ A Mate for Titan

The Feral Series
Book 1 ~ Hunger Awakened
Book 2 ~ Power Awakened

Demon Chaser Series (No cliffhangers)
Book 1 ~ Omega
Book 2 ~ Alpha
Book 3 ~ Hybrid
Book 4 ~ Skin
Demon Chaser Boxed Set Book 1–3

The Bride Hunt Series (Dragon Shifter Novels)

The Water Dragon Series

The Earth Dragon Series

Dragon HUNT

WATER DRAGONS BOOK 1

CHARLENE HARTNADY

CHAPTER 1

S he should be happy.

What was she thinking? She *was* happy.

Happy, excited and nervous all rolled into one. Nervous? Hah! She was quaking in her heels. This was a huge risk. Especially now. Her stomach clenched and for a second she wanted to turn around and head back into her boss's office. Tell him she'd changed her mind.

No.

She would regret it if she didn't take this opportunity. Why now though? Why had this fallen into her lap now? What if it didn't work out? She squeezed her eyes closed as her stomach lurched again.

"You okay?" Rob's PA asked, eyebrows raised.

Jolene realized she was standing outside her boss's office, practically mid-step. Hovering.

"Fine." She pushed out the word together with a pent-up breath. She *was* fine, she realized. More than fine, and she had this. The decision was already made. Her leave approved. She was doing this, dammit. Jolene smiled. "I'm great."

"Good." Amy smiled back. "Just so you know," she said under her breath, looking around them to check that no-one was in hearing distance, "I'm rooting for you." She winked.

"Thank you. I appreciate that," Jolene said as she headed back to her office, trying not to think about it. Not right now. It would make her doubt her decision all over again. She'd made the right one. The only thing holding her back was fear of failure. It was justifiable and yet stupid. She wasn't going to live with regrets because fear held her back. She was going to embrace this. Give it her all and then some. Her step suddenly felt lighter as she walked into her office. *Do not look left.* Whoever designed this building had been a fruitcake. This floor was large and open-plan. Fifty-three cubicles. There were only two offices. One was hers, and one was—*Not looking or thinking about her right now.* Both offices had glass instead of walls. Why bother? Why even give her an office in the first place if everyone could see into it?

It had something to do with bringing management closer to their staff, or the other way round – she couldn't remember. The Execs were on the next floor. *Not going there and definitely not looking left.* She could feel a prickling sensation on that side of her body. Like she was being watched. Jolene sat down at her desk and opened her laptop. Her accepted leave form was already in her inbox. She had to work hard not to smile. It was better to stay impassive. Especially when anyone could look in on her. This was going to work out. It would. All of it.

No more blind dates.

No more Tinder.

No more friends setting her up.

She was done! Not only was she done with trying to find a partner, she was done with human men in general. Jolene bit down on her bottom lip, thinking of the letter inside her purse. She'd been accepted.

Yes!

Whooo hooo!

It was all sinking in. She couldn't quite comprehend that this was actually happening.

The sound of her door opening snapped her attention back to the present. She lifted her head from her computer screen in time to see Carla saunter in. No knock. No apologies for interrupting. Not that Jolene had been doing anything much right then, but still. She could have been.

A smug smile greeted her. "I believe I'm filling in for you starting Friday for three weeks." Her colleague and biggest adversary sat down without waiting for an invitation. "Rob just called to fill me in."

"Yes," she cleared her throat, "that's right." Jolene nodded. *Don't let her get to you.* "I have too many leave days outstanding and decided to take them."

Carla folded her arms and leaned back. She seemed to be scrutinizing Jolene. It made her uncomfortable. "Yeah, but right now? You're either really sure of yourself or…" She let the sentence drop. "I believe you're going on a singles' cruise?" The smirk was back. Carla's beady eyes—not really, they were wide and blue and beautiful—were glinting with humor and very much at Jolene's expense.

It was her own fault. She should never have told Rob about why she was taking this trip. Why the hell had he told Carla? It was none of her damned business. *Stay cool!* She smiled, folding her arms. "I thought it would be fun."

"You do know that I'm about to close the Steiner deal, right? Work on the Worth's Candy campaign is coming along nicely as well."

"Why are you telling me this?" Her voice had a definite edge which couldn't be helped. Carla irritated the crap out of her.

The other woman shrugged. "It might not be the best time for you to go on vacation. Not that I'm complaining. It works for me." Another shrug, one-shouldered this time.

Jolene pulled in a breath. "I need a break. That's the long and short of it."

"Yeah, but right now and on a singles' cruise… do you really think you'll meet someone?" She scrunched up her nose.

"Why not? It's perfectly plausible that I would meet someone. Someone really great!" she blurted, wanting to kick herself for the emotional outburst.

"It's not like you have the greatest track record." Carla widened her eyes. Unfortunately, working in such close proximity for years meant that Carla knew a lot about her. In the early days, they had even been friends.

"But you should definitely go," Carla went on. "You shouldn't let that stop you," she quickly added. Her comments biting.

"I'm not going to let anything stop me. Not in any aspect of my life," Jolene replied, thrilled to hear her voice remained steady.

Carla stood up, smoothing her pencil skirt. "I'll take care of things back here. The reason I popped in was to request a handover meeting, although I'm very much up to speed with everything that goes on around here." She gestured behind her. "I'll email a formal request anyway." She winked at Jolene.

Jolene had to stop herself from rolling her eyes. "Perfect." She refolded her arms, looking up at Carla who was still smiling angelically.

"I need you to know that I plan on taking full advantage of your absence."

"I know." Jolene smiled back. "I'm not worried."

The smile faltered for a half a second before coming back in full force. "You enjoy your trip. Good luck meeting someone." She laughed as she left. It was soft and sweet and yet grating all at once. Like the idea of Jolene actually meeting someone was absurd.

That woman.

That bitch!

Stay impassive. Do not show weakness. Do not show any kind of emotion. She forced herself to look down at her screen, to scroll through her emails.

Two minutes later, there was a knock at her door. Jolene looked up, releasing a breath when she saw who it was. Ruth smiled holding up two cups of steaming coffee.

Jolene smiled back and gestured for her to come in.

"I was in here Xeroxing—our printer is down yet again – and thought you could use a cup of joe." Ruth ran the admin department on the lower level. Her friend moved her eyeballs to the office next door to hers. The one where Carla sat, separated by just a glass panel.

"You were right," Jolene exclaimed.

Ruth sat down. "Are you okay? That whole exchange looked a little rough."

"I thought I kept my cool. Are you saying you could see how badly she got to me?" Carla was all about pushing buttons. She only won if Jolene retaliated and she'd learned a long time ago it wasn't worth doing so.

"You looked fine. What gave it away and – only because I know you so well – was the way you tapped your fingers against the side of your arm every so often. I take it when 'you know who' said something mean." Ruth handed her the coffee and took a seat.

"Mean doesn't begin to cut it. Thanks for this." She held up the mug before taking a sip.

"What's going on?"

"Things have happened so quickly, I didn't get a chance to tell you. I'm going on vacation." Jolene briefly told her friend all about her real upcoming plans, as well as about what had transpired between Carla and her.

Ruth smiled. "I can't believe you're this excited." She looked at her like she had lost all her faculties. "It's not that big of a deal. Quite frankly, I'm inclined to partly agree with Carla, for once." She made a face. "Maybe you shouldn't be going on a trip right now."

"It's a huge deal, and you're right, I'm excited," Jolene gushed. "One in five hundred applicants are accepted, and I'm one of them. The shifter program is just the place for a woman like me. I'm ready to settle down, to get married and to have kids. Lots of kids. Four or five… okay, maybe five's too many, but four has a ring to it. Two boys and two girls."

"Two of each." Ruth chuckled under her breath.

She smiled as well and shook her head. "Actually, I'm not

too fazed about that. I just can't believe they actually selected me."

"You're nuts!" Ruth laughed some more. "Why's it so hard to believe? Just because you've had a bad run doesn't mean you're not... worthy."

"I'm thirty-four. I turn thirty-five in two months' time."

"And that's a big deal why?"

"Because thirty-five is the cut-off for taking part in the program." She had to undergo a whole lot of testing – including ones of the medical variety – and she'd been selected anyway. "I'm so done with guys running away as soon as they realize I'm serious."

"How is being a part of this program going to change anything? I love you long freaking time, but you do tend to scare men away. You're a little... pushy."

"I'm not pushy! I know what I want and I go after it. After everything I've been through, I'm not interested in anything less, and shifters actually want to settle down. They want kids. They want what I want. For once, I'm going to meet someone who doesn't run scared at the prospect of commitment and family." She sucked in a deep breath.

"Human guys also want commitment." Ruth raised her brows, taking another sip of her coffee. "They want kids."

"Just not with me they don't. None of them wanted anything other than sex or casual dating. Sure, they're more than willing to take the plunge as soon as they move on to the next one, but not with me."

"Have you ever stopped to consider that you're maybe coming on just a little too strong? You can't start out a relationship talking about marriage. Guys can't handle that."

"I'm not coming on too strong. I'm done wasting my time... that's all." Jolene took a sip of her own coffee, feeling the warm liquid slide down her throat. "I know what I want. Casual sex, endless dating..." She shook her head. "That's not it. Even living together. Have you ever heard the saying, 'why buy the cow if you can get the milk for free'? No... not for me. Never again!"

"You seem to think it's going to be different with a shifter. Can't say I know too much about shifters." Ruth shrugged. "Except that they're ultimately guys too."

"For starters they're hot. Muscular, tall and really, really good-looking."

"Okay, that's a good start." Ruth leaned forward, eyes on Jolene.

"They have a shortage of their own women, just like with the vampires. It's actually the vampires who are helping them set up this whole dating program."

"Oh!" Ruth looked really interested at this point. "No women of their own you say, now that's interesting."

"I didn't say no women, just not many women. Their kind stopped having female children, so there's a shortage. They have a natural drive to mate and procreate, which is exactly what I'm looking for." Jolene put her coffee down and rubbed her hands together. "I can't wait to get my hands on one."

"You might just be onto something here. Where do I sign up?" her friend whisper-yelled while smiling broadly. "I can't believe you told Rob you're going on a cruise. Where did you come up with that?"

"I shouldn't have said anything at all." She shook her head. "I don't know why I disclosed as much as I did."

"Yeah!" Ruth raised her brows. "I can't believe he told," she looked to the side while keeping her head facing forwards, "her."

"I know. Thing is, I've made up my mind. I'm going."

"That cow is going to move in while you're gone. She might just get the edge in your absence and take the promotion out from under you."

"I realize that, and yet I can't miss out on this opportunity. I'm willing to risk my career over this. It's a no-brainer for me." She sighed. "Don't get me wrong, I'm freaking out about it, but as much as I love my job, having a family would trump everything. I have a good feeling about this."

"Those shifters sound so amazing." Ruth bobbed her brows.

"I'll show you the website online. They only take three groups a year and then only six women are chosen each time. Just a handful from thousands of applications." Jolene's heartbeat all the faster for getting accepted. She was so lucky! Things had to work out for her. They just had to.

"You say these shifters are hot and pretty desperate?" Ruth smiled, her eyes glinting. "Why didn't you tell me about this sooner? We should have entered together."

"Not exactly desperate, but certainly looking for love. Ninety-six percent of the women who sign up end up mated… that's what the shifters call it, mated. It's not actually the same as marriage, it's more binding. Ninety-six percent," she shook her head, "I rate those odds big time."

"I can't believe you didn't tell me sooner." Even though she was still smiling, Ruth narrowed her eyes. "I thought we were friends."

Jolene made a face. "I didn't tell you anything because I didn't want to jinx it."

Ruth rolled her eyes. "I wouldn't get too excited until you get there. Until you actually meet them." Ruth snickered.

"With your luck, you'll get one of the bad apples."

"You shut your mouth. Don't be putting such things out in the universe."

Ruth looked at her with concern. "I don't want you getting your hopes up, that's all."

"Well too late, my hopes are already up." Jolene was going to win herself a shifter. Someone sweet and kind and loving. A man she could spend forever with. "I just wish it wasn't right now. This isn't a good time to be leaving."

"Not with that big promotion on the horizon." Ruth shook her head. "Not when *she* could take it."

"We're both on the same level. We both started at the same time. I hate how evenly matched we are."

"You're the better candidate though. I've never known anyone to work as hard as you."

"Carla works hard too. She's also brought in several big clients in the last couple of months, and she's not going on vacation. She'll be here day in and day out, whispering sweet nothings into Rob's ear."

Ruth made a face. "It's not like that, is it?"

"No, no." She waved a hand. "Sweet nothings of the business kind. It's still a threat just the same to me, and honestly, that's the only downside to this. I stand a good chance of losing to Carla if I go."

"But you are still going anyway." Ruth took a sip of her coffee, frown lines appearing on her forehead.

"I have to." She pushed out a breath. Hopefully, Ruth was wrong about the whole 'bad apple' thing.

Out now!

Printed in Great Britain
by Amazon